the Children
of the King

Sonya Hartnett is the internationally acclaimed
author of several novels, including
The Midnight Zoo and *Thursday's Child*,
winner of the *Guardian* Children's Fiction Prize.
She has also won the world's most
prestigious prize for children's writers,
the Astrid Lindgren Memorial Award.
She lives in Australia.

The Children
of the King

Sonya Hartnett

■SCHOLASTIC

Scholastic Children's Books
An imprint of Scholastic Ltd
Euston House, 24 Eversholt Street
London, NW1 1DB, UK
Registered office: Westfield Road, Southam, Warwickshire, CV47 0RA
SCHOLASTIC and associated logos are trademarks and/or registered trademarks of Scholastic Inc.

First published in Australia by Penguin Group (Australia), 2012
First published in hardback in the UK by Scholastic Ltd, 2014
This edition published by Scholastic Ltd, 2014

ISBN 978 1407 14357 6

A CIP catalogue record for this book is available from the British Library.

Printed and bound by CPI Group (UK) Ltd, Croydon, CR0 4YY
Papers used by Scholastic Children's Books are made from wood grown in
sustainable forests.

1 3 5 7 9 10 8 6 4 2

This is a work of fiction. Names, characters, places, incidents and dialogues are products of the author's
imagination or are used fictitiously. Any resemblance to actual people, living or dead, events or locales is
entirely coincidental.

www.scholastic.co.uk
www.sonyahartnett.com.au

For Frances

TWO MOST IMPORTANT
CHILDREN

She heard it: footsteps in the dark.

Cecily Lockwood, aged recently twelve, quailed in the darkness beneath her bed and listened to the steps coming closer. The curtains of her bedroom were drawn and only a ribbon of light nosed past the door, and sense told Cecily that she must be nearly invisible in the blackness: but she did not feel invisible. Her teeth bit her lip. Her heart bounced like a trout.

The footsteps had climbed the stairs. Cecily had heard the creak of each tread. The steps had come stealthily along the hall, pausing in each doorway. There'd been a silence when the steps reached her brother's room; Cecily had pictured Jeremy folded under his bed, his heart flipping and

1

diving. But no: Jeremy was too smart to hide under a bed. Jeremy would hide somewhere that could keep him secret all night. Only Cecily was silly enough to hide under a bed.

Now the footsteps had resumed. The rugs muffled them, but still they could be heard. Closer, closer – then a sudden bump, an *oof*. The steps had walked into the hall table. Cecily couldn't help but smile.

But the hall table stood just outside her bedroom, and it was abruptly too late to change her hiding-place for a better one. The door eased back on its hinges, letting in a shaft of soft light. Cecily held her breath, peeked past the bedspread's hem. The maker of the footsteps was carrying a candle, a long white taper taken from the dining table. Its flame cast a quavering circle of orange light. It radiated its glow on to the face of a man wearing a mask – a gas mask. The silvery goggles reflected the flame as a pair of burning pupils. The canister below them heaved like a horrible snout. At the sight of this monster, Cecily almost screamed. Almost.

The man stopped in the centre of the room. The candlelight grazed the rocking-horse, the hatstand, the shelf of china beasts. The masked head turned slowly to the window. The man was not puffing, but the mask made his breath sound like paper on fire. It took a single stride for him to reach the window. Holding the candle to one side, he felt amid the curtains. From beneath the bed Cecily watched, her heart denting the floor. When he didn't find her in the drapery, the man turned and pondered the darkness again.

2

She didn't need to hear him say, *I know you're in here.*

Three strides took him to the wardrobe. He threw back its door with a conjurer's flourish. Cecily nearly shrieked. She wasn't in the wardrobe, but she felt as if she was.

And now the man knew she wasn't in the wardrobe.

He turned painstakingly, on his toes. The hand that held the candle was spotted with white wax. A haze of candlelight fluttered over a wall. The flames that were the man's eyes fixed themselves on the bed. He had no voice, but Cecily heard him say, *Come out from under there.*

She could not bite back the tension any longer: she squeaked. Instantly the intruder dropped to the floor, flinging aside the quilt. The treacherous candle sent its rays on to the girl's aghast face. The man reached out a long arm, a hand dotted with wax. The hand closed on Cecily's wrist like a noose.

It was time to start yelling, and Cecily yelled. "Murder!" she bawled. "Kidnap! Help!" She struggled, grabbing at the bedsprings, but the hand dragged her from beneath the bed as easily as a pup from a drain. Tangled in dressing-gown, twisting eelishly, she plunged into the man's arms. "Kidnap, police, help!" she bellowed. She thumped his chest, the candle tipped, the man said, "Oof!" again. Cecily was only twelve, but she wasn't a twig. "Police!" she howled. "Monster! Murder in the dark!"

The man pulled off his mask. In the charcoal darkness Cecily saw his glittering eyes. "Found you!" he cried. "Now you're doomed, little girl! Any last requests?" And he wrapped his arms around her, and cuddled her like a lion.

"You're supposed to kidnap me, Daddy, play properly!" Nonetheless she ceased writhing and hugged him extravagantly. "Did you find Jem?"

"No." Her father clambered to his feet, hoisted his daughter to hers. "Jeremy wins again."

Jeremy always won – it was tedious. On the other hand, Cecily was always glad to be found. This game of hide-and-seek in the dark was thrilling, but also a touch hair-raising. "Jem!" she yelled. "You can come out now! He's found me!"

In the flurry of her unearthing a gap had opened between the curtains, and her father went to close them. He lingered a moment at the glass, staring down into the street. Cecily came close and looked too. Their house stood in a sweeping terrace of identically grand houses, each with pillars beside the front door and curved steps leading down to the footpath. Every house had a fence of iron spikes and rows of wide sash windows. All the gates were shut, all the doors firmly closed, all the windows taped and blackened. No lamp illuminated the footpath, no cars travelled the road. Every street in London was subdued, lit only by candles and the kindness of the moon. Cecily knew the banning of bright light was a good thing, intended to keep the city safe . . . but it frightened her. What the blackout *meant* frightened her. Her entire world was hiding in darkness, but not because it was playing a child's game.

4

Her father closed the curtains fastidiously. He looked down at his daughter, tucked a disarrayed curl behind her ear. "Come downstairs, Cecil-doll," he said. "There's something I want to tell you."

His child raised her face to him – a blue-eyed, slightly chubby and rather plain face, praised by her father as beautiful from the moment she was born. On this face was a frown. "Something good, Daddy?"

"Do I ever tell you anything that isn't good, doll?"

"No," she admitted.

Jeremy was standing at the top of the stairs, slender and moody in his pyjamas and dressing-gown. "Where were you hiding?" Cecily asked, but her brother would never give away such holy secrets and his only answer was to raise a haughty chin. This made no sense to Cecily, who said, "What's the point of hide-and-seek if you can't be seeked?"

Jeremy said, "Don't be stupid, Cecily. You're not *supposed* to be found. And you needn't scream like a lunatic when you *are*. You embarrass yourself. And *seeked* isn't a word."

Cecily chewed her cheek. "Daddy's going to tell us something," she bragged, but doing so did not completely quash the urge to push her brother down the stairs. One day, she was sure, Jeremy would be pleased he had a sister. That day had not arrived.

Their mother was sitting in the drawing room. It wasn't a cold night but there was a good fire weaving its tale behind the guard. A fire was necessary, as its flames lit the room and

5

made it cosy. It had come as a shock to many, and certainly to Mrs Heloise Lockwood, to discover that the blackout made velvet and silver and brocade and silk as comfortless as tin and tar.

"Daddy kidnapped me." Cecily flopped at her mother's feet.

"So I heard. I'm sure the man in the moon heard too."

"She doesn't play properly." Jeremy folded into a chair, radiating sourness. "She never plays properly. She hides in the most obvious places. She always gets found in five minutes."

Cecily rolled on to her back and blinked placidly at the ceiling. She had long ago learned that if she let her brother's grievances bother her, she would be bothered every moment of her life. "Cecily, you are crushing my feet," said her mother, so she moved lumpily aside. Their father was pouring brandy, and when he handed a glass to his wife the liquid caught the light and Cecily saw it swirl redly, as if stirred by the devil's finger. She asked, "What were you going to tell us, Daddy?"

Her father looked at her from his very tall height. He did not sit, which made Cecily realize that whatever he had to tell them was serious. She sat up.

"Children," he said, "you know why London is blacked out, don't you?"

It was a question insulting in its simplicity, and Jeremy narrowed his eyes. "In case of an air raid," Cecily obliged. "If planes come at night, they'll look for city lights. It will be

6

hard for them to see the city, if all the lights are turned off. But there hasn't been an air raid," she said – then, uncertain what an air raid precisely was, added, "Has there, Daddy?"

"Not yet, dolly. But we're sure there will be. The war has come very close to us now."

Cecily knew this, although she understood it, too, only vaguely. For weeks she'd heard talk of France falling, and while that sounded unlikely – how could a country, stuck firmly to the globe, fall or drop off? – she sensed that, whatever it was and however it could happen, it was grim. "I'm sad for poor France," she sighed. She'd been there several times and come home with nice souvenirs, so she felt its tragedy personally.

"The war is going to be bad for France," her father agreed. "It will be bad for us too. Already it's very bad, and it will certainly get worse."

"Humphrey," said Heloise.

"There's no point pretending otherwise, darling. This war has already been a rotten fight, and there's no acceptable end in sight. Thousands have died, and thousands more must, if we're to triumph. And at the moment, victory is no certainty. Indeed, at present it's looking increasingly unlikely. France has fallen, and logically we must fall next."

Even Jeremy, who relished such talk, stared in silence. The man who stood in the jagging light of the fire seemed less their cherished father than some craggy messenger sent up from Hades. "We won't, though." Jeremy spoke flatly. "We won't fall."

"We'll try our best not to. But we are fighting a strong and determined enemy."

"We are strong. We are determined."

"A mouse can be strong and determined. But not as determined as a cat."

Jeremy said, "We're not mice."

Cecily glanced at her mother, whose face was as stony as a marble Madonna's. Air raids and soldiers, fighting and dying, cats, mice: she wished she had someone's hand to hold. "Daddy," she said, "will we die?"

Her father turned his gaze to her, eyes that were the same shade of blue as hers but, in him, sharpened by years of deliberation and decision. For an instant these eyes seemed to see his daughter not as his child, but as his task. Then he said, "No, Cecil-doll, you are not going to die. You're going on a holiday."

Cecily's eyes widened, she saw the happy seaside, but her brother said crisply, "You're evacuating us?"

"It's best, son."

"No it isn't. Why is it?"

"You know very well. . ."

The boy sat up straighter. "Other people are staying."

"It's decided, Jeremy."

"What about school? I can't leave school—"

"Jeremy," said their mother, "please don't fuss. I don't want you here, where it's dangerous."

Their father spoke. "I've already kept you with me for

8

longer than I should have. My colleagues sent their families away weeks ago. But I've been reluctant: I don't want to be without you. I've been hoping events would unfold in such a way that you could stay. Unfortunately, the situation has worsened. The threat we're under is very real, children. I can't allow my selfishness to put you in danger. I couldn't live with myself if I became the cause of your suffering."

Jeremy and Cecily knew that the beloved voice, warm and mellow as pelt, masked a will of iron: the discussion was over and Jeremy knew it, yet he would not surrender. "What about you, Mother? If it's dangerous for us here, it's dangerous for you."

"I will be coming with you."

"And what about Fa?"

"Your father is staying in London."

Jeremy's blond head swung to his father. "Let me stay too. I'm not afraid."

"It isn't a matter of being afraid," his father replied. "I know you're brave. But it isn't safe, and I want you to be safe."

The boy stared. "I'm not a child."

"Please don't fuss," sighed Heloise.

"You're *my* child," said Humphrey Lockwood. "A most important child."

Jeremy kicked the chair. "But I want to stay! I want to help! I *can* help, Fa, I'm smart, I'm strong—"

"We're leaving tomorrow on the nine o'clock train—"

9

"Tomorrow!"

"– so go upstairs and decide what you want to bring. We might be away for some time—"

"How long? For the entire war?"

"Please stop shouting, Jeremy. Sometimes I believe you're worse than your sister."

Jeremy snapped his mouth shut. His eyes, which were a handsome deep-brown like his mother's, skimmed the shadowy spaces of the room. When he spoke, Cecily heard bitterness swilling through him. "It's not fair, Fa. You're *our* father, a most important father. Shouldn't you be safe too?"

"It's my duty to stay."

"But not mine?"

"You're fourteen years old, Jeremy. Your duty is to live to grow older."

Jeremy looked away. In the fireplace a burning log broke, showering the hearth with sparks. Cecily asked quietly, "Where are we going, Daddy?"

Her father turned from the son who was like those brilliant sparks of the fire, to the daughter who was as unremarkable as a daisy. Gratefully he told her, "You're going to Heron Hall."

A TEDIOUS TRAIN RIDE

Cecily sat with her forehead on the window, her eyes scrolled down so she could see the embankment rushing past as an endless grey smear. She tried to force her gaze deeper, to see the train's wheels and polished side and maybe the words painted there: *First Class*. But her eyeballs would swivel only so far and no further, depriving her of class and undercarriage; she sat back in the seat. She had some paper dolls and pencils for colouring them, as well as a book of puzzles, but nothing held her interest. Nothing could cage the birdlike flitter of her mind.

She remembered saying goodbye to her father, her arms around his neck. Though it had taken place only that morning, the parting was already a careworn memory. Cecily recalled crying, tears slithering down her cheeks . . . yet something had been strange. Inside herself, she hadn't wanted to cry. To leave her father alone in the imperilled city was such a desolate thing that tears felt oddly mocking. She'd longed to tell him the vital secret which would protect him through the lightless nights, but she didn't know the secret, so she had cried instead. Her father had had to jolly her, as if she were a baby. Cecily enjoyed being babied . . . but those tears had been shaming. Daddy had been left behind, and nobody knew when they'd see him again nor what trials he would endure before then: and through it all he would remember Cecily as a blubbering simpleton, never knowing that, inside, she'd wanted to be so much better.

"Stop," said Jeremy.

Cecily looked up. Her brother sat opposite, his hair a blond halo against the green seat. He was staring at the scenery and for an instant Cecily wondered if he was talking to the fields or the sun: *stop shining!* But he was talking to her. "Don't chew your nails. It's sickening."

Cecily shoved her hand under her thigh. She glanced at her mother, expecting flanking rebuke; but Heloise sat with her eyes closed, her face the marble Madonna's. *Dead*, thought Cecily. And hastened to add, *Please don't be dead.* She wished Jeremy had a habit she could likewise brand with that fierce word *sickening*, but her brother was not the type to forage in his nose or release ungentlemanly sounds, to do anything that risked lowering his towering dignity. Maybe that was her brother's failing, Cecily mused. He hardly ever remembered what their father, last night, had had to remind him: that he was just a boy.

She looked out the window. Green fields fringed with hedgerow, clouds casting odd-shaped shadows. Her thumbnail, incompletely chewed, was singing a siren's song. Knowing Jeremy was watchful, she thought of other things.

They'd taken a taxi to the station, a luggage van following like an elephant behind a black beetle. The station, when they'd arrived, had been startling. The cavernous building was always busy, but this morning it had been so crowded that Heloise had made the viper noise she usually reserved for Christmas. The crowd was of a kind such as Cecily had never seen. It was a crowd of *children*, all heights and ages, some dressed in good clothes, scrubbed boots and brushed hats, others in greasy rags. Some were chatting like parrots, casting grins here and there; others were sobbing into handkerchiefs knotted in their palms. Some held the hands of siblings, most carried gas masks, many of the younger ones clutched goggling toys. The children bumped against one another, touched their fingers to the sleek side of the train. Each gripped the handle of a satchel or small suitcase. On many of these cases the owner's name was written, and Cecily imagined a mother carefully printing out the words. Her own suitcase was too fine to write on; it had a leather tag.

Which brought her to what Cecily decided was the oddest aspect of this herd of children. Pinned to the lapel of every child's coat had been a cardboard tag exactly like a luggage tag or a price tag. Cecily was not so daft as to assume the children were for sale. She knew what they were. They were evacuees, some of the many thousands of the city's children being spirited beyond reach of the war into the countryside, just as she and Jeremy were being spirited. Unlike the Lockwood siblings, however, these children were not travelling in the company of their mothers to a place they knew and were fond of. There were several ladies among the crowd but they had the look of teachers, orderly, strict, aware – not the kind of ladies, Cecily sensed, who could be relied upon for a comforting word. These luggage-tagged children had been placed by their parents into the care of strict strangers to be hustled away into the unknown; and although it was for the children's own good, many of them looked as if their tiny hearts had broken.

Cecily bent her head. Heron Hall was far away, well past the lime-green fields and white villages that looked like something you could fit into your pocket. Their journey would not end for several hours. She thought about the children packed into the carriages behind her, the great weight of their bodies burdening the train. She wondered if they were sitting quietly or running about like wild dogs. How good it would feel, to run like a wild dog. Those no-nonsense ladies would doubtlessly demand best-behaviour, and only the baddest child would disobey. She wondered if the crying ones still wept.

There was a knock on the door and a porter looked in.

14

"Mrs Lockwood, may I get you anything? A magazine?"

"Thank you," said Heloise, "there's nothing," but rewarded him anyway with her watery smile. The porter nodded, the door slid shut. Cecily put her chin on the windowsill. The train continued to chuff its way north. Jeremy continued to stare out the window as if he'd rip the scenery to pieces. Cecily knew he liked the countryside – liked pacing about in wellingtons, liked wobbling an unsteady fence, liked discussing crops and animals as if he knew what he was talking about. It was evidence of the depth of his outrage, that he should stare at the friendly landscape as if he and it were mortal enemies.

Cecily could not help herself. She hated him to be cross. "Lambs." She pointed. "There's lambs." If there were lambs in these fields, there would be lambs at Heron Hall, full of bounce and silliness. Jeremy usually took a farmer's interest in them – how many had been born, how many were rams, which ones must be hand-reared, what price they would fetch. Now he said nothing; he seethed.

Cecily studied the ceiling, touched her nose with her tongue, twirled a lock of hair around a finger until the finger threatened to pop. She glanced at her brother. "Jem." Then, louder, "Jem?"

He heard twice, but looked up once.

"What do you think Daddy is doing?"

He gave her a glare that could have pickled onions. "Be quiet."

"Something serious."

"Be quiet!"

"Shh," said their mother.

"Well what was the point of the question?"

"Hush," said Heloise. "Leave her be."

Jeremy's gaze darted like a cat around the compartment. Only fourteen, he was not yet stern enough to smother into silence the storms which rose inside him. "I wish you'd let me stay home, Mother! What am I going to do at Heron Hall? What about school? You can't send me to the village school. If I stayed in London I could stay at school. Or I could do something – something—"

"Something what?" asked Cecily.

"Something worth doing!" her brother shouted. "There's a war, if you didn't know! Instead I'm being sent off to hide in the country like – like – a snivelling child!"

Cecily was of an easygoing nature, and rarely called anyone to account; but her brother's words rose a maternal hackle in her. "Don't say that!" she cried. "Those children aren't snivelling, they're frightened! You'd be frightened too, if you'd been sent away and you didn't know where you were going or what would happen to you!"

Jeremy was at a delicate age and in a tumultuous state of mind, but he was not naturally an unkind boy and he turned his face to the window, his cheeks dark with misery. Cecily looked at her mother, who had followed the conversation the way a beach-goer observes a squabble between gulls. "What

16

will happen to those children?" Cecily asked her.

"People will take them in. Don't fret."

But now that she was thinking about it, Cecily did feel inclined to fret. How tiny those evacuees must feel, how helpless! It seemed peculiar that the war, which was huge and serious and complicated, should bother to disrupt even the littlest life – like a tiger so bad-tempered it would crush a ladybird.

She looked at her brother. He was staring out the window. Quickly and stubbornly, she hacked off the last of her thumbnail. Jeremy continued to glare at the scenery as if his sister didn't exist. Cecily swallowed the nail, then retired to digest, tucking up her feet and closing her eyes. While she pitied the evacuees, part of her wished they had been on a different train so she wouldn't have had to see them and be weighed down by their plight. She had troubles of her own. She would miss her father, whom she adored. She would worry about him every moment of every day. She would miss Mrs Pope, who organized the house, and Mr Pope, who opened the door to invited guests and closed it in the face of all others. She would miss their good cook, Mrs Potter, and she'd miss her father's secretary, Mr Mills, who knew limericks. She wouldn't miss school, but she might miss her school friends. Most of them had been evacuated already, and not just to the countryside but to far away – to Australia and Canada, which were places Cecily had had to search the globe in her father's study to find.

She crinkled her nose. She was glad she wasn't going to Australia. She was glad to be going to Heron Hall.

Because that was one thing Cecily couldn't admit, not when everything was so dire, not with Jeremy being so tortured and Mama turned to marble, not when Daddy had been left behind and men were fighting and dying, not when poor France had fallen and London was too frightened even to turn on a light . . . no, under such circumstances it was wisest not to confess that she was delighted to be going to Heron Hall. Cecily loved Heron Hall. If the war lasted years and years, she wouldn't mind: not if it meant she must stay at Heron Hall.

She folded her hands and tried to sleep. The afternoon sun threw flares into the blackness of her closed eyes. Heloise turned a book's pages, Jeremy scratched the varnish on the windowsill. The train made a heavy rushing sound like a bull charging through shoulder-height grass. It hauled the children north, away from the menace of bombs, across squarely fenced countryside with its tidy woods and glossy fields and into a soundless place beyond it, where a white sky hung greatly over a silver land.

AVOIDING TROUBLE

The village station was usually a lonely place, having been built too ambitiously for the town it served; normally five or six souls wandered the oversized platform, and the distances between them could be so vast that they might each have been waiting for different trains on different days. Normally the busiest activity came from the swifts which ceaselessly skimmed the ornate roof, their rough dry nests crafted into corners, their chicks hidden from view.

But perhaps the grandiose station had been built, so long ago, for this singular day.

The evacuees poured from the train like an army. Large groups of children had already disembarked at two or three stations earlier along the way: now, at this grand station, the last and largest group was disgorged, wide-eyed and wittering. The ladies travelling with the children grasped wrists, pointed fingers, clapped forthright hands. In no time at all they had the evacuees in line, each child gripping the fingers of another, each suitcase by its correct owner's side. Caps were adjusted, hems were straightened, smudges were removed with a licked thumb. Then the ladies led this crocodile of mites out of the station and into the day, across the road and through the open doors of the town hall.

Cecily Lockwood stood surrounded by a wall of luggage, observing in silence as the crocodile disappeared head-first into the town hall. Heron Hall's car was waiting at the kerb, a luggage van standing behind it. Heron Hall was the kind of house whose car was never late – not because its owner, Mr Peregrine Lockwood, was particularly concerned about time, but because, around him, the world fell gracefully into place. The luggage had arrived all present and accounted-for, the afternoon sun was making a real effort to shine. Even Heloise had slightly thawed; she smiled at the porters, said, "Doesn't the air smell fresh?"

People, mostly women but also men, were following the evacuees into the town hall. As Cecily understood it, when they came out they would be in the company of a child, a chosen child, the one they would adopt for the duration of the war. While Heloise gave instructions to the porters about which cases to load first or most carefully, Cecily stared at the town hall, her eyes gobbling everything.

Women crossed the hall's threshold, some tentative, some eager. Some were village ladies, neatly dressed and clean. Others were farm ladies, also neat and clean. Some had friendly faces, some looked as if they'd been sent on a chore. Cecily thought of what would greet these women beyond the doors – the gazing faces, the red-rimmed eyes. Her heart strained on its leash.

Heloise believed she'd heard something shiver, so a box was opened and inspected. The dinner set inside was perfect, so it was a mystery. Heloise rewrapped each piece with care. "It's extremely expensive," she told the porters.

Then Cecily, watching closely, saw a woman come out of the hall. She was holding the hand of a curly-haired boy. He was looking up at her, and he forgot about the steps; but the woman held his hand and didn't let him fall. Cecily's heart thumped.

A minute passed, and another woman appeared. Behind her came a stunned-looking girl who had a grip on a younger boy. Two children! Cecily's heart flipped. She hadn't realized it was permissible to take two. If two could be taken, soon there would be nothing left. And now more ladies were gliding into the hall, friends laughing as though they were entering a tea shop for cake, and the woman with the curly-haired boy and the second woman with the siblings were disappearing down the street. Cecily's heart stretched its tether, she was suddenly more likely to fly than remain silent: "Mama!" she yelped. "Can we have a child?"

21

Heloise was not surprised to hear this. Her daughter wanted every homeless kitten and pup she saw. An encounter with a nestling fallen from its eyrie meant an afternoon of tears. "There's plenty of people who'll take them," she said. "Do not make a fuss please, Cecily."

Jeremy was standing by the car, having said nothing since disembarking beyond a greeting to Hobbs, Heron Hall's driver. Hobbs spent a lot of time poking about the fields in search of artefacts, and whenever he was at Heron Hall on holiday, Jeremy helped him. Last summer they'd found a small clay jar imprinted with the swollen face of a god; and inside the jar, besides dirt and ash, were countless miniature bones. Cat bones, said Peregrine Lockwood; finger bones, according to Hobbs. Jeremy had been silently watching the passers-by, the painstaking loading of the luggage, the comings and goings around the town hall. Now he spoke up. "We should take one, Mother."

Heloise paused; she always paused for her son. A gritty gust came out of the station and flapped the hem of her skirt. "Oh Jeremy," she said.

"We should. It's the right thing to do."

He didn't seem to be suggesting it out of kindness or to indulge his sister, but because it was *the right thing to do*. Nonetheless Cecily longed to jump at him, perhaps give him a little loving strangle. She resisted.

"Taking in an evacuee helps with the war effort." Jeremy touched a finger to a blot on the car's shiny bonnet. "If circumstances allow it, I don't know how one can justifiably refuse."

When Jeremy spoke in this high-flown manner, Cecily usually saw red. Now she held her breath and looked at her mother, who teetered with uncertainty. The breeze blew, and Heloise put a hand to her hat. "We're guests at Heron Hall," she said. "You would need Peregrine's permission. . ."

Cecily swung back to the town hall. People were stepping through its doors – not an unbroken flow of people, not a gushing crowd, but certainly a steady stream, and some of them were hurrying – and people were coming out. Beside them were one or two, even *three* children, in one case of greed. She sucked down a whimper, her heart kicked and squirmed.

Jeremy said, "Peregrine won't mind. He'd support the war effort. And we're not really *guests*, are we."

As they were in public, Heloise refrained from smiling. "Relatives are guests," she said. But her children knew she was recalling that coy fact which she never truly forgot: one day her son would inherit Heron Hall. They weren't guests: they were owners-in-waiting. "Oh, I don't know!" She dashed her hands to her sides. "Another woman's child. It's a responsibility. . ."

"Just a small one!" said Cecily.

"Everyone should do what they're capable of doing. Logically, people like us should take a dozen."

"A dozen!" Heloise looked at the porters, who were tying down the luggage, and at Hobbs, who was waiting patiently by the car. None of these obliged in sharing her alarm. "I don't think we could cope with a dozen!"

Jeremy shrugged. "I'm just saying what's logical."

A clump of townsfolk emerged from the hall, friends introducing their new children to each other, encouraging them to likewise be friends. "Mama!" Cecily squawked. "Just a little one? Please?"

Their mother was not the type to argue long, fearing it gave her wrinkles and aware from experience that she could turn her back on anything that came to displease her. "I suppose we can have a quick look," she sighed, which, when she said the same thing about toy shops, meant Cecily would get a new doll.

So Cecily bolted. She was halfway across the road when she noticed her brother wasn't following, and stopped. "Aren't you coming?"

Jeremy shook his head. He said, "Choose one who'll be your friend."

The town hall's doorway was a gaping mouth, a babble of voices coming from within. Cecily waited for her mother, took her mother's hand. The hall was a huge, high-ceilinged room with a stage at one end. Sitting on the wooden floor were the evacuees, their name tags dog-eared, suitcases by their sides. Among them walked ladies and gentlemen exchanging a smile here, a raised eyebrow there, as though the children were cakes in a fairground competition and the townsfolk were bakery judges. Among them too walked the ladies from the train, now carrying pens and clipboards. The hall was cold, as if winter

24

hibernated in this place while summer frolicked outside. Some children were crying tiredly.

A lady with a clipboard came up to Heloise. "Good afternoon, may I help you?"

Heloise gave her a martyr's smile.

Cecily didn't listen closely to what the billeting officer told her mother, nor to how her mother replied. Gazing about, she knew she'd never seen anything so strange as this sea of children. Some of them – the oldest ones, the ones who weren't smartly dressed, the ones not absolutely clean – were receiving only passing glances from the people, while in the far corner two men and two women were arguing over who'd been first to claim a cherubic boy. A small weeping girl was being soothed by her sister while a woman stood to one side, waiting to take the older girl away. "It's never easy," Cecily heard the officer say.

Most of the children, however, weren't crying. Some of them were whispering. Others were staring as dubiously at the adults as the adults were staring at them. Some slapped and pinched each other, some scowled and bounced their heels. Some rummaged in their suitcases. Many looked wanly terrified.

The billeting officer was smiling. "They don't all understand why they're here. And most of them would prefer not to be, of course."

"Do you think they'll be – difficult?" asked Heloise.

The official waved her clipboard. "There are always

troublemakers, aren't there? In every walk of life. Everything is being done for their own good, but not all of them see it that way. In general, however, we expect the arrangements to be happy. You'll get a lot of satisfaction from hosting a child for the duration."

Heloise stared doubtfully around the hall. The word *troublemakers* had made her flinch as if from a paper cut. She glanced at the doorway, but it was impossible to escape now. In this town people knew her face, had seen her trunks arrive, noted her entering the hall, would see her hurry away. All she could do was make the best of the situation. Because she tended to equate dirt with trouble, she told her daughter what many others had told themselves: "Choose a nice one. Not one of the . . . grubby ones. Not a . . . lout."

But Cecily, who was experiencing not an ounce of doubt, had already spotted the one she wanted, a child sitting composed beside a tartan-patterned suitcase. If this child had been a doll, she wouldn't have been locked in the glass cabinet, accessible only with the shopkeeper's key. She wasn't particularly well-dressed or special. But her bobbed black hair was silky and her skin was clean, and in her blue eyes was a glint that looked painted there by a toymaker in a mischievous mood. Cecily sidled close, chirped, "Hello!"

The girl's eyes were not the insipid blue of morning, but the cobalt of tropical birds. They watched Cecily warily. "Hello."

"What's your name? How old are you?"

As if her identity had been recently changed, the girl glanced at her tag. "May Enid Bright. I'm ten."

"I'm Cecily Lockwood. I'm twelve."

May Bright nodded, but not as if this was interesting.

"Do you have brothers and sisters, or are you here by yourself?"

"Just me," said the evacuee.

Cecily hugged her coat. Everything felt good. "Would you like to come and stay with us? My uncle has a house in the country, that's where we'll be living. There are sheep and chickens and a cow, and a dog named Byron. I have a brother, Jem, he's fourteen, he's outside. He's all right, not horrible. . ." She petered out, rummaging for words which she sensed were not there: for the first time in her life, Cecily discovered she didn't actually know how to get what she wanted. She had never pleaded or negotiated. Everything had simply arrived. The realisation made her feel a bit shipwrecked. "You'll have lots to eat," she tried, "and a big bed to sleep in."

May Bright nodded again; but the glint in her eyes suggested she could live off scraps and sleep soundly in hay, and that Cecily needed to do better. Taxed, Cecily looked around, at the questioning adults and answering children, at the falling-down socks and the jetsam of luggage and the creased identity tags. There was a smell to match the sight – unaired clothes, stale bread – and a sound as well. Fists on boards, shuffling paper, a toddler's trenchant whine.

27

"I have a lot of toys," she offered, "but you can play with them. I won't mind. I wouldn't even mind if you broke them. I'd know you hadn't done it on purpose."

"I don't break things," said the evacuee.

"Oh, I do." Cecily sighed. "I'm a clumsy-clot. Once I broke a football. How do you do that?"

The raven-haired child gazed at her without smiling, perhaps wondering if she too would fall to pieces in the care of this lummox. All around them children were being escorted from the hall, hands waving, tears dropping. Spaces were opening up on the floor, leaving circles like vacated nests. Soon there would be little choice left for both those who would take, and those who would be taken. Without a word the evacuee reached for her case, and Cecily brightened. "So you'll come?"

"Yes," said May, as if it wasn't really anyone's business. "I will."

A MAN LIKE A MAGICIAN

The nicest sound was the crunch of gravel beneath tyres as the car swept on to the carriageway of Heron Hall. The journey had not been long, but Cecily, bundled between May and her mother, worn down and over-excited, had felt every mile as a torment. She wanted the travelling to be done. She wanted to step into the quiet world of Heron Hall. She wanted to show off to May Bright. As they passed through the ancient gates and along the elm-shaded drive, the girl put a hand to the window as if not truly believing what she saw, and Cecily felt the satisfaction of a goddess placing a newly crafted human upon the earth.

Quite suddenly the arms of the elms parted, and there stood Heron Hall. A three-storey manor built of sandstone and countless panes of glass, the Hall was surrounded by pastures which rose and fell mellowly, and by copses of beech, oak and yew. The land was threaded by a river and its many rivulets, and after rain the ground became spongy and burped bubbles. Sturdy sheep grazed the fields, and navy-blue swallows chased each other up and down the dips of the land.

Standing before the Hall's front doors was a dog as black and shaggy as a bear, with clear ambitions of becoming the same size as one. "Byron!" Cecily scrambled from the car as the animal loped down the steps to meet her. Jeremy, in the front seat, turned to May. "I hope you're not scared of dogs?" he asked.

"I'm not scared of anything," said May.

The housekeeper, Mrs Winter, met them at the door. She was not typically a soft-hearted woman, but when told the small stranger was an evacuee she said, "Poor pup, we'll take care of you." Cecily beamed; it was all going swimmingly. "Where's Uncle Peregrine?" she wanted to know, but her mother said, "Wash and dress first, you're not presentable," and sent the children upstairs with a wit's-end flick of her hands.

The staircase was grand, very wide at its foot, much narrower at its peak. It was like climbing a polished mountain. Cecily hauled herself up by the banister, beckoning the evacuee along. When they reached the summit of the landing, the window showed a view across pastures coloured like a bruise, purple and yellow and green. Daylight was waning, evening was near.

Jeremy and Cecily had been coming to Heron Hall all their lives, and each had a favourite bedroom they considered their own. May Bright followed Cecily along the passage, her blue gaze taking in everything. She bumped into Cecily when the older girl stopped. "This is mine." Pushing back a door revealed a spacious room with a carved fireplace and a rose-coloured quilt on the four-poster bed. A fire had been lit to take the chill off the air, and on the dresser stood a vat of water beside a folded towel.

May peeked around the doorframe. "Pretty."

"It's lovely! I bet you've never seen such a lovely room. I bet you've never been inside a house as grand as this, have you? You must feel like you're having a dream. You could have your own bedroom, but you'll probably want to share with me. They'll bring a little cot for you and put it in the corner."

"Can I have my own room?"

Cecily looked at the girl. "Don't you want to share?"

"Well – at home I have my own room. I'm used to it."

Cecily had envisaged the two of them tucked up at night, giggling and whispering until sleep claimed them. It was disappointing to have the vision extinguished, and she wished she hadn't given her guest the choice. "I'll tell Mrs Winter."

"My suitcase is in the car. Shall I fetch it?"

Cecily, whose affection for the evacuee had taken a knock, felt a healing surge of fondness for her. "Someone will bring it, don't worry about things like that." Suddenly charged, she made a swooping run into the room, flying like a cannonball on to the bed. "Somebody will *bring it*! Haven't you heard of staff? Don't tell me you don't have them at your house?"

It was an ugly thing to say, and Cecily knew it. She held her breath and glared at the ceiling as the girl crossed the room. Her legs were thin and her feet made no sound when they touched the floor. She stopped at the window and scanned the horizon. In the fireplace, something popped. "There's a lake out there," she remarked.

"Heron Lake," said Cecily dully. "Where the herons live."

"I've never been to the country."

"What?" Cecily rolled on to her stomach. "Never?"

"I once went to the beach for a holiday. But never to the countryside."

"Amazing!" Cecily genuinely thought it was. Everyone she knew passed at least a few weeks of each year in fine houses dotted around the landscape, riding ponies, eating too much, taking strolls, growing bored. It was a pleasant thing required to be done. "I feel sorry for you."

"I liked the beach." The girl curled a knuckle on the glass. "My family doesn't have lots of money, like yours does."

It was a new sensation for Cecily, to feel awkward about being well-off. Once again she wondered if she'd made a bad choice in evacuee. "I can't help it. It isn't my fault. Anyway, some people are much richer than we are. Compared to some people, we're *poor...*"

May said, "I can fetch my case, I don't mind."

"Somebody will bring it!" Cecily blasted it like a bellows. "They have to – they always do – it's the rule!" And buried her face in her arms. May Bright seemed a cranky kind of child, the type who listened too closely to what was said, who asked a lot of questions and made it necessary for a speaker to think before speaking: the future felt utterly spoiled. Perhaps the girl could be exchanged, or maybe it was safer just to return her and go without. Kindness to strangers evidently carried no guarantee of being repaid. Deflated, Cecily's thoughts went to her father, left behind in the city. She pined for him already, and grew a little fishy-eyed. The sound of footsteps saved her from further subsidence – she leapt up and darted into the passage, accosting her brother at the top of the stairs. "Are you going down to see Uncle? You're not presentable! Mama said we had to bathe first!"

"Mother's not in charge of the world," Jeremy replied, in the tone of one who's just realized it. He stepped past his sister, who watched as he descended the staircase in strides. Mother would be cross yet Jeremy wasn't bothered: Cecily was impressed. Her brother had gone a bit odd today, and she liked this new version of him. Brimming once more with the joy of existence, she caught May by the wrist and dragged the evacuee down the stairs before the child had a chance to further spread her gloom.

The main rooms of Heron Hall opened off the entrance hall and then, in a maze of doors and passages, off one another. Cecily hurried her charge through them, not pausing to explain. As they neared a particular door, however, she tweaked the child to a halt. "Now don't be afraid," she warned portentously. "Uncle Peregrine won't hurt you. Just answer what he asks and don't say anything else, all right? Don't talk about being rich or – or – about *anything*, all right?"

"All right," said May.

"Don't ask where his wife is. He had one, but she died. She died, and their baby died, and now he's all alone. So don't ask about his wife and baby, all right?"

"All right," repeated May.

"And don't say anything – *impolite*. You know what impoliteness is, don't you?"

"I do."

"Good," said Cecily. "I want to be proud of you."

Byron met them at the door. His huge head, black as coal, was as silkily soft as a duckling. May's hand disappeared in the depths of his coat. "Hello dog," she murmured.

It was a snug room they entered, one of the smallest and most homely of the rooms in Heron Hall. Its sky-grey walls were covered with paintings, and books and papers were scattered about, as were small puzzles and interesting objects, carved curios, carriage clocks, a typewriter, a gramophone. Underfoot were flattened rugs, and a fire karate-chopped at the throat of the chimney. There was a good smell of cigarette smoke mixed with toast and dog; this room was a den, the lair of Heron Hall's owner. Here, rather than in any of the grander rooms, was where the house's living was done.

"Uncle Peregrine!" Cecily bounded forward to bob and hop before a man who stood by the mantelpiece. She would have pounced on him, but that was not allowed: this was a gentleman who preferred not to be rough-housed. So Cecily confined her greeting to this little loving dance, and her uncle smiled in a bemused way and said, "Good evening, Cecily."

Jeremy was settling in an armchair, and Heloise Lockwood was seated, less relaxedly, on a striped sofa which sprouted dog hair. Neither of them looked thrilled to have the girls in the room. Cecily turned adoring eyes to her uncle. "Are you pleased to see me?"

"Slightly," he said. Cecily grinned; another day she might have bombarded him with chatter about blackouts and air raids, about leaving Father and the journey on the train and the crocodile line of children, but to set an example for the evacuee she chose to behave less like a hurricane and more like a young lady. "Look what we've brought with us," she said, wagging a hand to beckon the newcomer. "This is May Bright. She's been evacuated from London. I chose her at the town hall – just like picking a kitten from a basket!"

May Bright released her grip on Byron's coat and stepped nearer to Mr Lockwood. Her host at Heron Hall was, in appearance, like a wily criminal from an adventure tale. He was tall and lean, and his face was shadowy, and he wore his dark hair long, like a mane, which May had never seen a real-life man do. His eyes, too, were very black, as if only night-time sights were invited into them. There was something mysterious about him, something beyond the fact that he looked like a sly magician, beyond his wife and baby having died, beyond his intolerance of questioning. There was something about him that made you feel he knew more about you than you did. If he'd had a weasel up his sleeve, a knife in his belt, or the ability to change into a jackdaw, none of it would have surprised.

Standing before such a man, no handshake or how-do-you-do seemed fitting. Instead, May did an unusual thing: she bowed. She bowed low enough to see Peregrine Lockwood's feet, which were clad in sloppy brown slippers.

Cecily screamed. "Oh, she's bowing – stand up, you silly thing! You don't have to bow – Uncle Peregrine's not the king! Mama, did you see – May bowed!"

"Hush!" hissed Heloise, whose cheeks nevertheless turned rouge on the child's behalf.

Jeremy, however, didn't laugh. He, too, honoured Peregrine. And when May lifted her gaze, she saw that Peregrine wasn't laughing either. He said, "You are a welcome guest in this house, Miss Bright. I hope we can keep you safe."

Cecily used her brains and stopped chortling, and made herself as overlookable as possible by plumping down beside Byron at the end of a sofa. May huddled by the dog's head and the two girls shared patting duties as the conversation, interrupted by their arrival, resumed.

Peregrine said, "So Humphrey finally decided it was time you left London. I was starting to wonder what he was waiting for. A submarine chugging up the Thames, perhaps."

"Humphrey is my father," whispered Cecily to May. "He and Uncle Peregrine are brothers."

"He shouldn't have done it," said Jeremy.

Peregrine looked at his nephew. "You think you should have stayed?"

"Not Cecily and Mama – they should be here. But I could have stayed with Father. I'm not a child."

Heloise said, "It's good of you to have us, Peregrine. I'm concerned about Humphrey, of course, but I'm glad we're finally here."

"Humphrey knows how to take care of himself."

"It's a necessary thing for someone in his position to know. But I can't help feeling that this war will soon put every man, woman and child in peril. No corner of the world will know peace."

"Then why have we come?" asked Jeremy. "If it's not safe anywhere, I should have stayed home—"

"Jem, don't be rude!"

"I'm not being rude—"

"Don't be wilfully obtuse, Jeremy. For the time being, we're safer here than anywhere."

Peregrine said, "I shall tell Mrs Winter to keep a truncheon at the ready."

Heloise looked wounded. "You may laugh, Peregrine, but it's not funny. In fact it's bleak and terrible. France has fallen. This nation stands exposed on every side. Anything could happen now. Invasion. Occupation. Our way of life torn apart by strangers. Our future in such awful, awful hands—"

"Let's be quiet!" Cecily smacked the floor. "That's enough now! May is getting frightened."

Peregrine's eyes lighted down like two hawks. "Are we scaring you, May?"

"She's not scared." Jeremy craned to see past the wing of his chair. "She's not scared of anything."

Alarmed to find herself pulled into the discussion and, worse, made its central object, May changed the subject. "My father went to France," she offered.

The statement cooled the room. "Your father's a soldier?" asked Peregrine.

"He wasn't before the war, but he became one."

"He volunteered?"

"Yes, volunteered."

"France!" said Cecily. "Are you very worried about him?"

"Of course she's worried about him! Don't be thick, Cecily."

May glanced around at her adopted family, who gazed back as if she were a most exotic thing. When she spoke, it was carefully. "My mum says being worried can't change what happens. It can't make things better. So you should just live and – be happy about what's good. That's what I think, anyway."

Cecily stared, impressed by this windfall of wisdom. At home on quiet evenings she had sometimes watched her brother and father playing chess, and this conversation had been like one of those games, and May's contribution was the calm surprising move which Daddy always encouraged Jeremy to play. Peregrine looked at his sister-in-law and said, "I'm sure Humphrey and his friends will be disappointed you don't trust them to keep us safe," and Heloise answered, "Oh, men! I've lost all faith in them." To which Peregrine laughed in a charmed kind of way, and the discussion was finished; and it was difficult to tell who had triumphed, and who had been forced to lay down their king.

There was a tap at the door, and a maid announced, "Dinner is served for Mrs Lockwood and the children."

Peregrine looked at his guests. "I hope it's not too early to eat? Mrs Winter thought you'd like an early dinner after your long day. It's lamb, Cook tells me. The last lamb the butcher's apprentice slaughtered before he signed up, apparently."

Jeremy said "Huh", in an exhaling way; Cecily thought that anything which stopped the lambs being slaughtered couldn't be a completely bad thing. Heloise rose, plucking at wisps of dog hair. Jeremy slipped across the room to open the door for her. Cecily kissed Byron's brow and unfolded her dependable legs. In the doorway she paused: "Aren't you coming, Uncle?"

"No," he said, and added, "I hope you'll be happy here, May."

And May, although it was grossly impolite, didn't reply. Mr Lockwood had stepped away from the fire and it was only now that she saw her host walked with a limp. She smiled daftly and was yanked into the passage by Cecily, who hissed hotly in her ear.

"Don't speak! Don't say anything. He had polio when he was a boy. Do you know what polio is? It's a disease that makes people crippled. Don't mention it to him, that's very bad manners. But you can't catch polio, so you mustn't be afraid."

The consistency of her courage had been much questioned over the course of this endless day. Yet again May vowed, "I'm not afraid."

"This is a good house, you'll like it here—"

"I know."

"So you mustn't act shy and silly, not ever. Shy people are just irritating. And you mustn't be scared of Uncle Peregrine. I know he's not what you're used to, but—"

"I like him," said May.

"Good! But don't bow to him again, all right? *That* was peculiar. You looked like a little drinking bird."

"Hmm," said May.

"Now let's dash, or we'll be late for dinner. Cook doesn't like lateness. Timeliness is the rule!"

"Let's go then," said May. "I'm fast like a whippet."

Cecily stepped back, cocking her head. This evacuee she'd chosen was certainly bizarre, but at some unrecognized moment she had decided to keep her. "What are you smiling about?" she asked; and suddenly snuffles of laughter were swelling in her nose and plumped out her cheeks. "You're going to bow again one day, aren't you?"

"Maybe." May shrugged. "If I'm in the mood."

Cecily giggled so much she had to cover her mouth. It had all been precarious and could have gone badly, but now things promised to be fine.

M IS FOR MISCHIEF

Dawn came early in those short weeks of summer. The sun rose limpid over the hills, pale and tired despite its youth. Its heatless light reached over miles of marsh, crept across streams and slunk over rocks, cast thin shadows from robins and shone dimly off dew, and finally crawled, with a daddy-longlegs's fragility, up the walls of Heron Hall to Cecily's window, there to stare through the glass like a starved cat. Morning was here.

Cecily stretched beneath her rose-coloured quilt, her mind a pleasant field of emptiness. Heloise had done nothing about sending the children to school, and ten days of idleness had wiped Cecily's brain almost clean of thought. She lived each hour as if she were a corked bottle adrift on the sea, with no demands upon her except to present herself three times daily to the table. There was, of course, the matter of the evacuee, who was prone to bouts of independence and required supervision; but Cecily had taken to the role of instructor with ease, and found it hardly any bother to be constantly criticising and instructing.

"Breakfast," she said.

Heron Hall had never been a warm house, not for a single day of its long existence, and certainly wasn't now, in summer. Cecily hopped up and down while she dressed. She listened for sounds coming from elsewhere in the house, perhaps the noise of tureen lids and cutlery, but apart from the thudding of her feet, silence reigned. That could be changed.

Beyond her bedroom, the passage showed a row of shut doors. There was only one she'd dare to open, and she did so without knocking.

May's room was the same size as Cecily's, and its wallpaper of green vines and its view over the orchard were pretty; but it couldn't be as nice a room as Cecily's, so she believed it was not. The bed was large – too large for such a scrap of girl, who disappeared into it as if into a quagmire. It was often easiest to locate the child by squeezing the bedding until it protested.

"Wake up! Breakfast!"

She prodded the bedclothes, rifled cold air beneath them, tamped them down firmly, finally threw them aside. The bed was empty, May was gone. Cecily sighed.

It wasn't the first time the evacuee had absconded. On their third morning at Heron Hall she'd left her room without waiting to be officially freed. The girls had had a quiet talk about it, if a talk can consist of one party talking and the other party not. Cecily had warned of the perils inherent in an old house. There were doors that might lock, staircases to fall down, statues that might topple, loaded pistols who-knew-where. "It's best if you wait for me," she'd told May, and although she didn't specify the parameters of the waiting, she meant *always and at all times don't do anything without me*. Cecily simply did not like the idea of May Bright, who was only a guest here, rambling about and making herself at home. It could lead to tragedy. And it wasn't right.

Gratifyingly, May had agreed. "All right," she'd said. And then she had blithely continued to do exactly as she liked. Some mornings she stayed in her room, reading in bed or even sleeping in it; on others she'd been discovered chatting to the maid in the kitchen, fetching preserves from the cellar, brushing Byron on the doorstep, standing on tiptoe to inspect a tray of butterflies. On the mornings she went roaming, she could be found anywhere.

And now here she was again, gone.

Cecily looked about as if the room knew where the girl had got to, and would confess under a sufficiently stringent glare. Cecily had helped May unpack her suitcase, so she knew exactly what belonged to the girl and felt also that these things belonged to herself. On the dresser lay May's hairbrush and a blue ribbon rolled up like a snail. Stacked behind these were the three novels of her library, each dated the day of the evacuation and inscribed with the words *"love, Mum"*. Beside them lay a piece of paper and a pen: Heloise had written to the child's mother on their first day at Heron Hall, and May had soon sent a letter of her own, and evidently she'd started another. *Dear Mum*, Cecily read, *I hope you are well. I am well. The weather here is not too warm. I miss you. I think about Dad a lot.* As the epistle ended there, so did Cecily's reading: she turned her attention to a box of barley sugar from which she prised a yellow twist. She didn't expect to find May in the dresser, but she opened the drawers anyway. Folded in the top drawer were the girl's stockings, knickers, handkerchiefs and slips. In the middle drawer were her petticoat and cardigan. In the bottom drawer were her gas mask and identity card. Nothing of interest. The room stood vacant and cool, its walls a tangle of vines. Cecily's reflection wavered in the mirror, a chubby-cheeked girl with a veil of yellow curls and eyes of the most timid blue.

She crunched up the barley sugar and raided the box for another.

In the cupboard hung the dun dress which the evacuee had worn on the train; she had another made of summery cotton, and a third made of thick wool. This last was missing. Missing, too, was the girl's overcoat. "She's gone outside," the detective deduced.

She went downstairs and through the maze of corridors

at the back of the house. Fragrances came from the kitchen, beckoning Cecily to its door. Cook was sitting alone at the table, reading the newspaper with her back to the stove. It was a perfect opportunity to order breakfast and have Cook prepare it without distraction, so the tea would be sweet, the toast without char, everything served just as Cecily liked it, pipingly hot and divine. But Cook had a nephew who was fighting abroad, and instinct warned Cecily not to interrupt a woman who was scanning a list of names for one she recognized. Besides, the longer May Bright was rambling about unchaperoned, the more necessary it became to reel her in. The longer she survived by herself, the less she needed Cecily to be with her. Breakfast must wait.

A quick check in the mud room confirmed the evacuee's wellingtons were gone.

The rear of Heron Hall let on to a cobbled yard where horses had once been hitched into carriages. Standing to one side was a stone barn, inside which were the coach-house and stalls. There were no horses at the Hall any more, for Peregrine did not ride; the milking cow spent the winter in the barn, but it was summer now and she was out in the field. But buried within old piles of straw could be found nests of mice or chicks, and doves cooed in the rafters; in summers gone by, Cecily and Jeremy had often played in the stalls, and Cecily had introduced them to May with the air of Moses parting the sea. The girls had spent happy hours here: but a quick investigation showed the child wasn't in the barn this morning, not unless she was buried like a rodent in the hay.

A row of sandstone outbuildings stood further back in the yard: here were the knife-house and the grain-house, the lumber-house and the gardener's store. Here too was the outside privy, which was a fascinating black hole to the centre of the earth. Cecily checked each of these, certain she would discover her errant charge in one or the other. May liked flowerpots and seeds, she liked bent nails and vats of corn, she liked the Hall's grumpy gardener, she liked Hobbs the driver and the flashy long-nosed car, she probably liked knives and lumber, for all that Cecily knew. But the outbuildings were empty, and although the pitch-dark privy was the sort of place some people felt drawn to, May was not there either.

At the end of the outbuildings stood the kennels. Generations of hounds had lived in them, but Peregrine did not hunt, and Cecily had only ever known the kennels as a collection of empty cages into which she'd once shut herself and pretended to be a dog. That was a long time ago, but she hadn't forgotten the look on her mother's face when she discovered her daughter baying like a beagle. "May?" she called now, nose to the wire; and only a breath of breeze answered, light-footed as a fawn.

A low stone wall surrounded the yard, and its railed gate stood ajar. Cecily gazed at it, and through it to the meadow beyond. Cecily liked being in the country, but she was no great fan of the actual *countryside*. Contact with the land inevitably resulted in feelings of damp, cold, and weariness. But in the past ten days she had learned that, rather than avoid such feelings, May Bright seemed to like them. Staring at the unhooked gate, Cecily knew, with a sinking heart, that this morning the evacuee had struck out alone into the wild.

She climbed the gate's railings most cautiously, and surveyed the fields.

The morning sun wasn't strong enough to take the chill from the air. The breeze carried the clean odour of soil and trees. The countryside around Heron Hall always seemed contrary and undecided – it was rocky and boggy, flat and hilly, flowery and thorny, balding and overgrown, purple, yellow, green, grey, brown, and sometimes it was all these things within the space of a few footsteps. It was rough country, scratchy with heather, crunchy with stone, whispery with running water and gusting leaves. In winter it snowed here, but the land stayed wet even through the brief summer, and patches of mud lay in wait for Cecily's boots.

She shielded her eyes and looked into the distance, over the fields to where hills rose half-heartedly and fell away. Jeremy had once found a ring in the shadow of those hills: Peregrine said it was a gentleman's ring dating from Tudor times, and had let Jeremy keep it though it was too big for him. Since they'd arrived at the Hall, Jeremy had spent most of the days roaming the estate, a mackintosh over his shoulders and a little earth-pick in hand. In the mornings he read the newspapers and in the evenings he listened to war reports on the radio, frowning past the spitfire of static. As company he was useless, preoccupied by unshared thoughts, preferring, if he could not be with his uncle or with Hobbs, to be alone: while he seemed to like the evacuee, it was unlikely that wherever Jeremy was, May was too. Yet anything was possible, and Cecily knew herself not to be canny. She didn't always notice everything, even things which were plainly before her, and she'd come to expect the world to surprise. Usually, the surprises were good. Maybe that would change. Maybe Jeremy and the girl had gone off together, this cool morning, to dig up the mouldy skeleton of a medieval monk. Everyone would make a fuss and forget completely about Cecily.

"May!" she hollered, and the breeze snatched the word and whisked it away. She rubbed her face, groaning. It was possible the girl had gone to the henhouse or to the lake where the herons prowled. She might have skirted the Hall and gone down to the road and along it to the village, although there was no good reason for anyone to go there. The shops wouldn't open for another hour. If she'd gone to the road, it would be for a reason other than shopping.

Cecily wobbled on the gate, wishing her father were here. He would cut through this confusion and speak sense. *Cecil-doll*, he might say, *it's no good worrying about other people. You've got to look after yourself.*

She took his advice and climbed down from the gate – just

as a shadow romped from the darkness of a distant copse of trees. It romped, and it barked – it was Byron. The dog's blurred shape was followed by another, small and swathed. Cecily watched the girl pick her way over the changeable earth; and as Byron, sighting her, ambled up sloppy-tongued and sodden of paw, and as it became clear that the child had merely been out for a walk, Cecily's anxiety hardened into crossness. "I was worried about you!" she shouted, when May was close enough to hear.

"Why?" the girl shouted back.

"I thought you'd drowned in the lake!"

"Why?" May replied.

Cecily clamped her mouth shut: she wouldn't enter a thankless conversation. She watched the girl toil over the unpredictable terrain, her hands held out for balance. It was not in Cecily to hope somebody would slip and break a leg, but the evacuee deserved at least a reprimand. "You're not allowed to leave the house before breakfast," she told her.

The breeze had reddened May's white cheeks, and whitened her red lips. Her black hair shone blue, her blue eyes sparkled like sapphires. Her hands were smirched from touching trees, and her wellingtons were stuck with leaves. "Why?" she asked.

"Cook doesn't like it, that's why. Cook gets angry. Look at you, you're filthy, you'll have to wash, and change your clothes. Where have you been?"

"I went for a walk—"

"Well you're not allowed to—"

"Why?"

"Stop saying why! Uncle Peregrine wouldn't want it, that's why!"

May wiped her nose. "I don't think Mr Lockwood would care if I went for a walk," she said.

"He wouldn't!" snapped Cecily, who wasn't skilled at fibbing. Honesty was, for her, not merely the best policy, but the only one she could reliably manage. "I was worried," she said again.

May answered, not unkindly, "You don't have to be. I'm used to looking after myself."

"In the city, not – *here*!" Cecily waved a hand at the landscape as if there resided dragons. "Where did you go?"

"I followed Byron. We found a big stream."

"You mean the river? That's far."

"How can it be a river? It only came up to my ankles."

"I don't think there's a law to say how deep a river should be," Cecily said archly.

May chose not to argue. "We crossed the river, and we found some old ruins."

"Those ruins! It's dangerous there. You could have been lost or killed. Probably killed."

"Killed how?"

"A stone could have fallen and smashed your brains, ninny!"

"Huh." May was impressed.

They had followed Byron into the courtyard, May's

boots leaving prints on the cobbles. While Cecily's back had been turned to the house, the curtains had been opened in the drawing room and Cook had put out a saucer of milk for the cats. Cecily registered this as a good sign: Cook would not be feeding cats if she'd found her nephew's name in the newspaper. The world had righted itself, all was as it should be. "What *are* those ruins?" May asked.

"Just some ruins. They were once a castle, maybe for – a knight? Ask Uncle Peregrine, he knows. He knows things about – history."

"Is he a historian?"

"No. . ." There was a problem, Cecily didn't know exactly what a historian was, or if her uncle was one; and if he wasn't a historian, she didn't know what he was. "He reads a lot of books. He knows all sorts of things. I know he sends telegrams to Daddy, and Daddy sends telegrams to him. Something to do with the war, I expect. Everything's to do with the war. It's no use asking me, I don't know anything, and what I do know – I forget."

May smiled. She wasn't a particularly smiley child, indeed she wore a serious expression almost always; but she smiled at Cecily like somebody who could read a person's thoughts. It was a worrying revelation, and also a relief. But then she said, "Look at the stripy kitten – oh Byron, don't chase him!" and Cecily decided she'd smiled because of the quaint animals, and was both disappointed and reassured.

LIVING IN IGNORANCE

May appeared at the table with clean clothes and face, the dewdrops brushed from her hair, her nose no longer blanched. No one would have guessed she'd spent the first hours of the day fording rivers under the gaze of ravens.

Peregrine Lockwood was already at breakfast, as were his niece and nephew. Heloise had breakfast brought to her bed, an indulgence for which the at-table diners had a low opinion. But her absence meant they ate without formality, forgoing the fine dining room for a small round table in a room that seemed to have no purpose except to catch the morning sunshine with its windows, and beam warmth and light on to its occupants. It was a lovely room, a sleepy room, a room which smelt of hot bread.

May slipped into her chair opposite the master of the

house. He was perusing a newspaper and didn't look up. He said, "You stole my dog."

"I didn't. . ."

"He claims you did, extremely early this morning. He says he was on guard as usual outside my door, but that you lured him away with hypnotism."

May smiled. "He wanted to come with me."

Peregrine turned a page of the newspaper. With his wild hair and white shirt turned back at the cuffs, he looked a lot like a pirate. "It's his word against yours. I'd believe a dog before a child."

"You went out this morning?" asked Jeremy.

"What's her punishment, Uncle Peregrine?"

The pirate glanced sideways. "Only criminal minds turn to punishment, Cecily."

"But she stole Byron! She should be punished."

"Perhaps her punishment could be to watch you eat a soft-boiled egg."

Cecily was baffled. Her uncle knew she hated soft-boiled eggs. "You should keep quiet," her brother advised. "Where did you go, May?"

"Only to the river."

"You thought it was a stream! She thought it was a stream."

The maid brought in a rack of toast and fresh tea, and asked the evacuee what she would like. "A soft-boiled egg!" yipped Cecily. And May, who hadn't yet fully embraced the luxury of ordering whatever she chose, shrank in her chair and mumbled, "A soft-boiled egg, please."

They shared the toast and passed the marmalade. Sunshine purred around the room, sprinkling stars of light on the silver pots and cutlery. Through the tall windows the breakfasters could see chaffinches and starlings hopping on the lawn. The room faced the front of the house: out there was the gate, the road, the town, eventually London followed by the world. Peregrine folded the paper and passed it to his nephew. "Debacle," he remarked.

"What does that mean?"

"*Debacle*. A noun from the French, meaning utter collapse, a point at which we haven't quite yet arrived, but very soon might. Cecily, your ignorance is repellent. Don't they teach you anything at school?"

"They try, but it doesn't stick."

"Perhaps because you're never there. Why aren't you? There's a school in the village."

Cecily shrugged. "Mama hasn't sent us."

"I won't go." Jeremy sliced his toast savagely. "What's the point? A poky little village school won't teach me anything I don't already know."

May's boiled egg arrived, accompanied by toast; Cecily grunted, "Ugh!" when decapitation revealed the yellow syrup inside. Sunlight sparkled on Jeremy's hair as he scanned the front page of the newspaper. Reports of the war barked across it in sooty print. "Debacle," he agreed.

"If it's just going to be a debacle," opined his sister, "we shouldn't fight it. We should stop before it all gets silly."

Peregrine looked sharp at her. "Absolutely and without question we have to fight. We had to fight, and we have to keep fighting."

"But if it's a debacle, and soldiers are being killed. . ."

"The consequences of not fighting would be worse. May's father knew that; it's why he volunteered." Peregrine chose a pear from the bowl, halved it with the glide of a knife. "Soldiers have died and many more will die, there's no doubt about that. But there are times when men's lives can't matter as much as what they must be used for."

"For victory!" shouted Cecily.

"Don't shout!" said her brother.

"Yes," agreed Peregrine, "for victory."

"Is victory more important than anything?" asked May.

"Not always," said Peregrine. "But in this case, certainly." To which the small girl nodded.

There was a knock, and the maid brought in the post, several envelopes for Mr Lockwood and a parcel each for the Lockwood children. "Oh!" Cecily gasped. "From Daddy!"

May cleaned out the contents of the eggshell while the parcels were opened. Humphrey Lockwood had sent a book of Shelley's poetry to his son and a gold bangle to his daughter. With each gift came a letter in an envelope; Jeremy tucked his letter into his pocket but Cecily tore hers free and read. "*Dear Cecil-doll, I hope this letter finds you happy, and not thrown down the privy by your brother. No doubt by this time you are running Heron Hall with efficiency, and perhaps giving Peregrine cause to wish he'd never been born. Home is very quiet without you, but I am getting a lot of work done without interruption. I miss you Dolly, and enclose this bangle which I hope will remind you of me. I saw it in a shop window and it seemed right to buy something pretty when everything is so serious. . .* Oh, Daddy," she sighed, sliding the bangle on to her arm. "Poor Daddy. What did you get, Jem? I got a bangle. Look, it's lovely."

She twirled her wrist so the gold caught the light. "It suits my white arm," she decided. She looked at May. "Still no letter for you, May?"

"No."

The kindness of Cecily's nature rose up to give her trouble. "Maybe your mum was busy. I'm sure she'll send something – maybe tomorrow?"

"It's all right," said May.

"And if not tomorrow, probably the next day. She wouldn't have forgotten you – not yet."

"Cecily! Leave her alone."

"It's all right," repeated May.

But it was a sorry sight, the evacuee and her eggshell amid the ribbons and wrapping; it caused Cecily pain. A distraction occurred to her: "Uncle Peregrine, May was asking about those ruins by the river. What is that place? I've forgotten."

57

"Snow Castle. You should be careful there. Ruins can be dangerous."

"That's what I said! Didn't I, May?"

"*Snow Castle*." May mused. "It sounds like something nice to eat."

"That's not its real name though, is it?" Jeremy folded the paper and put it aside. "That's just what local people call it."

Peregrine sat back in his seat, taking his teacup with him. Walls of sunlight boxed him in, making his chair a throne. "The true name of the castle isn't known," he said. "Flimsy things like words become lost in time. But some say the castle never had a name – that it was always a castle of no name. It was built at least five hundred years ago, maybe a hundred more."

"Golly," said Cecily.

"Hardly golly at all," her uncle replied. "Old castles aren't rare. Every well-to-do person's house was a castle in those days, there were lots of them around. Most are ruins now, just broken stones and a few crumbling walls; even most of the grandest ones are lost. What does make Snow Castle unusual is the fact that much of its stone is marble – snow-white marble, originally."

"So whoever built the castle must have been someone grand."

Cecily swung to May, curls bouncing. "How do you know?"

The girl, challenged, blushed a little. "Marble comes from Italy, where Michelangelo lived. So only a rich person could bring it all the way here and use it to build a house."

Peregrine smiled. "How do you know that, May? Do you have an interest in architecture?"

The evacuee blushed pinker. "My dad taught me things."

"Is your father an architect? An artist?"

"No; but on weekends we used to go to the museum to see the paintings and the stuffed animals and the fossils, and he used to tell me things."

"I'm scared of those stiff animals." Cecily boggled her eyes.

"The animals were my favourite," said May. "We always visited them first. I like the walrus. Then we see the mummy in the sarcophagus, he is Dad's favourite. I like the mummy too. Then we visit the icons and the head-hunters, and after we've looked at everything we. . ." She paused, glanced up.

"You what?" asked Cecily.

The girl seemed to have forgotten what she meant to say. Then she spoke with a start. "We'd get ice-cream if it was a warm day, and chips if it was cold."

She looked down at her plate. Peregrine Lockwood ate the last slice of pear, contemplating her. Jeremy said, "The land around here is full of artefacts – Iron Age metal, Roman glass. We'll go digging if you like, find a gift for your father."

Jealous Cecily said, "What would anyone want with a

bit of old glass? Look, May, I've got an idea: we can share this bangle. I'll wear it today and you can wear it tomorrow, and I'll wear it the next day and you—"

"It doesn't matter." May raised her head. "You keep it, Cecily."

"It suits your white arm," said Peregrine.

"So if he isn't an artist, what does your father do, May?"

"Before the war he was a school teacher."

"A teacher." Peregrine sighed. "And here you are, brain turning to mush."

"She learned about Snow Castle," Cecily pointed out.

Peregrine scoffed. "There's a lot more to Snow Castle than those few facts. There's an entire terrible legend around that castle. Some people say it is called Snow Castle not because of the stone it's made from, but because its story is as hard as winter."

"Really?" Jeremy's eyebrows rose. "You've never told us this before."

"I have not. You are children, and the tale is cruel. Unfit for childish ears."

Jeremy made a face as if he'd never heard such rubbish. Cecily said, "You can tell us a cruel story – we're brave! May's not scared of *anything*, remember?"

"Tell it, Uncle Peregrine."

The master of the house shook his head. "It's a very long story, and I'm too busy for long stories."

"You don't do anything except read and write letters!

That's not being busy."

"I'm busy thinking."

"Thinking about what?"

"Things such as the past and the future."

"*Those* aren't important!"

"Then give us a clue," said Jeremy. "Is the castle haunted?"

"Every castle is haunted. Hauntings are as common as cats. Ghosts are nothing to fear. It's *real life* you should worry about."

"So the story is about real people?"

"Yes, real people."

"Children?"

"Some children, yes."

"So it's a true story," said Jeremy. "It's history."

"I cannot vouch for its absolute truth, but it is certainly history. The story is almost as old as the castle itself."

"Five hundred years old!" Cecily's mind swam.

Jeremy leaned forward, scheming in his eyes. "Uncle Peregrine, what if you told us the story in pieces, just a bit now and then? That way, it wouldn't take up too much of your time. And if the story is history, we'd be learning something – it wouldn't matter that we're not going to school."

"Good idea!" cawed Cecily. "Then I wouldn't be so stupid!"

Peregrine considered them, sipping his tea. The children watched him, intent as collies. His nephew knew his weakness: Peregrine Lockwood was clever, and like all clever people he liked to share his cleverness around. Yet he would not concede easily: "You'd whine when it became scary."

"We would not!"

"You'd wake up screaming in the night."

"We never would!"

Peregrine turned to May. "You're the wisest child at the table. What's your opinion?"

May said, "My dad used to tell stories."

"And he's not here now," said Cecily, "so you'll have to tell them instead, Uncle Peregrine."

The man looked closely at the girl. "Would you like that, May?"

May's fingertip circled the rim of her glass. "Yes," she decided.

Peregrine sighed, as if much put-upon. "I suppose even a little education is better than none," he said. "I cannot promise an instalment every day, mind you. I am not at your beck-and-call, and unlike you three loafers, I have things to do."

Triumphant Cecily squiggled in her seat. "Tell it!" she screamed.

"No." Peregrine placed his cup on its saucer, dusted his hands and pushed out his chair. "Now I'm busy. Tonight, after supper, we will begin. In the meantime, I wish you good day."

He limped from the room and left them sitting at the table, their young faces buttered with sunshine, the last piece of toast standing, a lone soldier, cold on the rack.

A SECRET IN THE CASTLE

Cecily lost sight of her protégée after breakfast, having gone to the bathroom to wash jam from her cuffs and returned to find May, whose cuffs were never jammy, absent-without-leave for the second time that morning. She ran through the house feeling not angry or disappointed but like a child in a department store who has turned to discover itself separated from its mother. One after another of the big rooms proved empty, however, and finally Cecily stopped, confused. A puzzled part of her put forward the idea that she'd invented the evacuee's entire existence.

Byron barked, far away. Cecily spun like a rabbit and ran.

By the time she reached the cobbled yard, May and Byron were already way across the field, heading in the direction of the woods from which they had emerged that morning. "Wait!"

Cecily shouted. "Wait for me!" She ducked past the gate and hared off over the grass, gratified to see that they'd heard and halted and were looking back. She could not understand why they hadn't simply waited for her in the first place.

The earth was still slithery with dew, and the girl and the dog were further away than they had seemed – Cecily was puffing when she reached them. "Where are you going *now*?" she panted. "Back to those old ruins?"

May said, "You don't have to come."

"No, I'll come. I need some exercise. At school we used to do exercises every morning. Star jumps – like this! I didn't like it. Why are you carrying that plate?"

May was holding a dinner plate over which she'd draped a kitchen cloth. The cloth bulged with whatever lay hidden beneath it; Byron could not tear his eyes away. A thin breeze was blowing, and it blew strands of hair across May's white face. She said, "Let's go into the woods so they can't see us from the house. Then I'll show you."

Cecily glanced back to Heron Hall. From this distance the house looked half its proper size. She and May would be, from its windows, tiny kewpie dolls on the landscape. She looked at her shoes, which were new and now splattered with muck and torn grass. Nothing was good: yet Cecily was a follower, and she followed her companions at a clump.

There were too few trees – pallid alders with spindly arms, brawny ash with fleshy leaves, oaks as monolithic as Nordic warriors – to make a true forest; but frothy thickets of shrub and bracken grew between the trees, and the copse was thick enough to disappear into, and to hide Heron Hall from view. It was shadowy and still beneath the branches, and a dark bird flew clatteringly away. May wove through the undergrowth until the meadow beyond the woods was visible and sunlight was nosing the shade. Cecily was about to whine, "Aren't you going to show me?" when the girl stopped, looking up at her with treasure-chest eyes.

"Can you keep a secret?"

"Of course!" Cecily huffed, although it was obvious to anyone, and certainly to May, that secret-keeping would tremble at the very edge of Miss Lockwood's abilities.

Nevertheless the evacuee balanced the plate on one hand, and drew the cloth away. On the plate were breakfast leftovers: the last slice of toast and two eggs, a scarlet lump of blackberry jam and a greasy knot of butter, a scorched pikelet and, pride of the collection, a very chill-looking omelet. "I took it from the kitchen when Cook wasn't looking."

"I won't tell. Why do you want it?"

"Promise again you won't tell."

"I promise-promise!"

"There are two boys hiding in Snow Castle," said May.

Cecily absorbed this. She had always liked boys, and having a brother meant she knew a lot about them; but part of what she knew was that boys could have a rough, unpleasant side, and not merely the unpleasantness of Jeremy in his moods. Driving with her father around London's streets, she'd seen boys of the wilder kind throwing stones and chasing each other, kicking fences and wrestling on the ground. She had no desire to make the acquaintance of boys like that – and boys who'd hide in ruins seemed likely to be the kicking kind. "What are they doing? Are they playing? Are they local boys?"

May said, "Wait and see."

Cecily wasn't absolutely sure she wanted to see; but she was no shrinking violet, and it would be humiliating to watch May march off unaccompanied, as she appeared certain to do. May Bright, Cecily was discovering, was not cautious. Perhaps it was because of all the museums. Places like that encouraged adventure and curiosity – too much, in some children.

They struck out over the field with Byron in the lead. With Heron Hall hidden by the woods behind them, it was easy to imagine they were utterly alone on the earth but for a few distant sheep who raised their horned heads to watch the dog trot by. The breeze made Cecily's thoughts go to the overcoat she'd left on a hook behind the laundry door. To break the silence she said, "Parky, isn't it? I wish I'd worn my wellies. Mama will be cross if I ruin these boots."

May, who wore both coat and wellingtons, glanced at her companion's feet. "You can wear mine."

"But then you'd have to wear my boots. They'd still get wet and dirty."

"I'll wear bare feet," said May.

Cecily baulked to discover she was keeping company with a barbarian. "You'll step in sheep-do!"

66

"Sheep-do is just chewed grass."

Cecily had rarely walked barefoot out of doors; May probably did it as often as she could. Cecily both envied such feet, and did not want to share their shoes. "My feet won't fit your little boots," she said. "Forget it."

"What about your mother getting cross?"

"Oh, she's always cross, I'm used to it. She's always nice, but always cross. She lets me do whatever I want, but everything I do annoys her. She scolds me for being spoiled, but buys me lots of things. That's funny, don't you think? You *can't* be sad and happy, but you *can* be mean and nice."

"You can be happy and sad," said May. "I am."

Cecily looked at her reverently. "Are you sad but happy because your dad is a soldier?"

May creased her nose. "I'm always sad and happy about lots of things. It's just the way I was made, I guess."

Cecily grinned. Words came irresistibly to her. "Sometimes I want to pick you up and squeeze you," she said.

"Everybody does," sighed May.

The conversation had carried them downhill, and the earth had become rockier; they stepped from platter of stone to gnarly mound, from gravel bank to nest of shards, avoiding slimy rockpools in which mosquito larvae writhed. Soon they heard the piano-music of water – the river. A dragonfly veered in for a close look at Cecily, making the girls giggle. It was lovely to be rambling through fields with the convalescent sun rubbing their brows, with swallows skating the tufty earth and a river to intrepidly ford. London with its blacked-out windows seemed far away, forgettable.

The river, when they came to it, was shallow but broad. Byron waded across, saw that the children hadn't followed, and waded back again on dripping paws. May and Cecily considered the rushing water. Rocks rose from it randomly, a higgle-piggle of stepping-stones. May looked at Cecily. "I could carry you?"

Cecily snorted at the vision of the evacuee squishing beneath her like an ant into the riverbed. There was only one person in the world who'd be permitted to ferry her over the water, and that was her strong father. He being absent, Cecily took to the stepping-stones, and despite much wobbling made a fair job of the crossing, soaking just one stocking.

The river flowed in the basin of a steep ravine; when they'd climbed the far side, the girls saw the ruins.

Snow Castle had once been big – bigger than Heron Hall, although, as Mr Lockwood told them, not big by the standards of the time when it was built, when *big* meant astonishingly *huge*. Nonetheless it had been a castle, with all that this implies: it had had towering walls and turrets, beams as great as trees, arched doorways wide enough for processions to pass through, ceilings so cavernous that owls had nested in them. It had had wings and ramparts and thin windows from which to shoot arrows, internal courtyards, banquet rooms, hidden doors, secret passages. It had had a chapel and, in its bowels, a dungeon.

It had housed sculptures and paintings, tapestries and cushions, carpets and carvings, its fortressed heart had been clad in gilt, silver, glass, gold, damask, ivory, ermine.

Now nothing but the barest remnants of that palatial past remained. The roof was gone, and what was left of the walls stood like tombstones in a neglected burial-ground of the titans, rising from the earth as skewed and shapeless as brawlers' teeth. Some walls were gigantic, taller than trees; others were stunted as crones. Some had their stained faces turned to the sun, and cast hulking shadows behind them; other walls stood in these shadows and had done for centuries, and wore coats of festering slime. In many places the walls had collapsed and disappeared almost entirely, leaving only ragged stumps, knee-high, overgrown, to show where rooms had been.

And all around where the great castle had stood were hillocks of the hefty stones which had built it, no longer snow-white but the dull colour of dishwater, littering the ground and sinking gradually into it. Weeds grew around the toppled blocks, and insects made homes in them, and at night foxes used them as lookouts from which to yell hoarsely across the hills. On many of the stones could be seen traces of the mason's tools that had cut them, but these scratches were the only sign of human hands. Nothing had survived to speak precisely of the people who had made this place their home: the paintings were vanished, the ermine was dust, only imaginings were left of the gold.

Cecily called Byron closer. "These boys who are here . . . are they scary boys?"

"I don't think so. They're gloomy."

"Gloomy!" It sounded harmless, even hilarious; still Cecily kept hold of the dog. Side by side the girls and the hound pushed through the grass, edging between the heaps of stone until the castle loomed above them, and they stopped.

"Hello?" called May.

Nothing living moved, not a sparrow or a fieldmouse; the hem of the kitchen cloth wavered in a breeze that wasn't strong enough to rustle the wiry weeds. But the castle spoke: it answered them. *Hello*, it said. *Hello.*

Cecily glanced up – she thought she'd glimpsed movement at the peak of the highest wall. A weed was growing from a crack there, flurrying gently, but that wasn't what she thought she'd seen. She had had a sense of flatness and falling, like a lean bird coming to land. She flexed her fingers around the dog's collar.

"Hello?" May called again. Her voice hurried through the castle and returned to her, *hello hello hello.* "I've come back – hello?"

Nothing. Then suddenly Byron's ears stood upright, and in that instant Cecily saw too.

TWO VERY HORRID BOYS

A boy with a dainty, melancholy face was peering from around a corner in the disintegrating heart of the ruin. The sight of him made May chirp, "It's me!" and start forward between the fallen blocks. Carefully, Cecily followed.

The boy edged out from the protection of the wall. "Who's that?"

"That's Cecily, she—"

"I don't like strangers." He said it almost to himself; then more forcibly, as if convinced. "I don't like strangers! Stay where you are! This is wrong, this is – a betrayal!"

May stopped, the plate tipping. "Cecily's my friend. It's all right, you can trust her. Look – we've brought some food."

"You needn't have. We didn't ask for it. Don't presume to know what we want. What we want, we'll ask for!"

Cecily, emboldened by indignation and the presence of the dog and the title, rarely-worn, of *friend*, rose to her full height, which was as tall as the boy and broader, and thundered, "Excuse me! My uncle owns this land. You are a *trespasser*. We're not horrible girls, and we're not being horrible to you, so you'd better not be horrible to us, had you? Otherwise I'll tell my uncle, and *then* you'll be in trouble!"

The boy stared as if she'd walloped him with a plank. "Your uncle owns this land?"

"Yes he does!"

"Then he must know we're here. . ."

"I don't think so. He's very busy. He doesn't have time to wonder if horrid boys are hiding in the castle. But I could tell him – and I will, if you don't behave!"

The boy's face, which was already pale, became, for an instant, almost watery; and Cecily had an odd awareness that he was always unwell, and tetchy and sensitive because of it. "I'm sorry," he said, and it wasn't only pride he had to overcome to say it, but an impulse to cry. It didn't make her pity him.

"You should be. It's hateful to be rude." Cecily released Byron's collar but the dog stayed by her, his coppery gaze on the stranger. "We can be friends, but not if you're going to be unpleasant. Who else is here?" she asked.

The boy looked into the shadows. "Brother. Come out."

From behind a wall, unhesitating, stepped a younger child. If the boys were indeed brothers, the first must have taken after one parent, the second after the other, for they did not look much alike. One seemed a collector of stamps, the other a player of rough games. The younger's face was not wary but cheerful, his frame not gangly but robust. Both of them, however, had pretty, dove-grey eyes, and both of them wore their mousy curls long, all the way down to the collar. It took Cecily a moment to remember who else kept their hair like that, in a lion's mane, and realized it was her uncle Peregrine. And Cecily, who knew a bit about clothes, saw that those the brothers were wearing – linen shirts, velvet jackets, leather boots, calf-length cloaks – were well-made and costly, and something else as well, something she couldn't immediately define. "Hello," she said to the child. "What's your name?"

"You don't know who we are?" The older boy was surprised. "You haven't heard of us?"

"No. . ."

"You haven't heard us mentioned? Not by anyone here-abouts?"

"No!" Cecily had to smile at these brothers with pretensions to fame.

The boy considered a moment, then nodded seriously. "Good. If you don't know who we are, I'd prefer not to say. I keep this secret not for us, but for you. The less you know, the safer you will be."

"Tongues tattle!" trilled the child.

"Safe?" Cecily scowled. "What do we need to be safe from?"

73

"There are ears everywhere – I beg you, lower your voice. There are eyes peeking round every corner. Watchers," said the boy. "Spies."

May and Cecily exchanged the glance of bemused tolerance that young ladies have for grandiose young men. "I don't think anyone's *spying* on us—"

"You don't know. There are many places a spy might hide."

Cecily conceded it was certainly the case that throughout the ruins there were many crannies from which someone who had absolutely nothing better to do might spy on them. Jeremy perhaps, or some village children, or maybe . . . the police. Maybe the police were looking for these boys. They seemed peculiar enough to warrant the interest of the police. To find herself in casual conversation with two felons brought all Cecily's cunning to the fore. "If you won't tell us your names, we better not tell you ours," she said.

"We know your names," said the little one. His childish voice was smug and annoying. "She's silly May, and you're silly Cecily. We see you! We hear you, chatter chatter chatter! Silly Cecily, with a wet stocking! Sounds like a song."

"Shh," said his brother, but not harshly – with love.

"And that is silly Byron, a dog," added the child.

There were many people who had permission to tease Cecily, but these two were not among them. She said nothing, but her gaze darkened. It was May who spoke. "We brought you some breakfast, in case you're hungry."

She drew back the cloth from the plate. A lifetime had passed since the toast had browned, since the omelette had slipped sizzling from the pan: the leftovers, cold and jostled, looked like the slops that get tipped into a trough. "Oh!" said the boy.

"They're trying to poison us," snarled the child.

May blinked at her mutant offering, swallowing hard. She stood on tiptoe to sit the plate on a ledge of stone. "I'll leave it here. You can eat it later, if you're hungry."

"Take it away! We'll never eat that. I'll tell our mother you're trying to poison us! She'll make you sorry."

This was too much for Cecily. "Where *is* your mother? I'd like to speak to her."

"She wouldn't like to speak to *you*."

"I think she would. I think she'd like to know that her son is awful—"

"She won't mind. She'll laugh."

"Then your mother must be awful too!"

The child gasped as if stabbed. "Don't say such things about my mother!"

"I'll say what I like!" Cecily roared. "You need a good pinching, you do!"

The child sprang forward, hair flying; he screamed, "Just try it! I'll fight you!"

His brother weighed him down with a hand. "Stop. Remember your manners. What did I teach you?"

The child hopped about, seething like a snake; gradually,

reluctantly, simmered. With the air of repeating a disbelieved mantra he stated, "Living among peasants shall not make us peasants. Living in wilderness will not make us wild."

"Behave as Mother and Father would wish. Apologize."

"I'm sorry," he said, clearly not.

"I'm not a peasant." Cecily spoke like a shelf of ice. "My father is rich and important."

"Not as important as us," retorted the brat.

"Brother," said the elder, "you are shaming me before our guests."

"Ah!" The child's grin broke. "I am sorry. I am sorry now."

May smiled, and maybe she forgave the brothers their appalling behaviour: but Cecily never would. A younger sister, the softer-hearted sibling, she was accustomed to making peace: but she did not have to forgive these boys, and she never truly would. She made her tone affable, her expression friendly; but she sat down on a pile of rubble and made Byron sit beside her, and set about teaching the trespassers who was, and who wasn't, king of this castle. Pinning her glare on the older boy she asked, "Why are you hiding in Snow Castle?"

"Is that what you call it? I am surprised. To name a place makes it exist . . . and this place does not. Perhaps that's why we are here: because this place does not exist."

The breeze blew, the girls stared. The boy was evidently sophisticated, with his words like poetry. Perhaps he hoped to scare them off with his depths. It would not work. Cecily, used to the world speeding past her, had long ago cultivated the patience of a labrador. The only way to get rid of her was to give her what she wanted. "Why are you hiding?" she asked again.

"We're not *hiding*." Though the younger boy was sturdily made and burdened with bad temper, there came from him a sense of lightness, as if he itched to zip round the fields like a hare. "We're *here*," he said, "you can see us, we're standing right here."

"We were sent here," said his sibling – there was lightness about him too, Cecily noticed, the vagueness of the physically fragile which seems to place them just barely on the earth. "We had no choice."

"We don't *want* to be here." The child sighed. "We *want* to go home."

"Oh!" Suddenly everything made sense, as if Cecily had turned a corner in a Maze of Mirrors and stepped out into the real world. "You've been sent up from London, haven't you?"

"Yes, sent here—"

"And you've left your mother behind in London – just like you did, May! Did you come up on the train?"

"They brought us here against our will—"

"Against our will!" snapped the youngster, like a turtle. "I yelled and kicked and fought and screamed, I didn't want them to take us anywhere! But nobody cared."

77

"And now they're keeping us here, in this nowhere place, as if we are nothing but – prisoners."

"I saw grumpy children like you at the station," Cecily reminisced. "I wondered if you were running around on the train like wild dogs. It was sad to leave home, I know that, but London is in danger. . ."

"London has dangers," the elder agreed.

"My daddy will make it safe again, though," Cecily couldn't help adding. "May's dad, too. Is your father fighting in France?"

"Our father is dead," said the boy.

"Oh!" May clutched her hands. "Did he die in the war?"

"No. He survived all battles where mere men were his adversary."

It sounded impressive, but the small child was grudging. "He shouldn't have died. He should have lived. Everything went wrong after Father died. Now the bad men have sent us to this place, and I don't know where Mother is, and nobody is a friend of ours, and these horrible peasant-girls are here! Everything's wicked! Wicked!"

This was the last straw for Cecily. Staggering to her feet she shouted, "You don't understand anything! It's all for your own good, you stupid boys! My daddy will save you and us and everyone, and then you'll be sorry for saying what you just said! Come on, May, let's go. I'm going to tell Uncle Peregrine these stupid boys are here, and he'll come and chase them off with a gun!"

"How dare you!" bellowed the child, darting back and forth with a robin's agility. "How dare you shout at us! How dare you call us names! Get away from us! You're wicked!"

In the excitement Byron started barking, a sound fearsome enough to make trees sway and land slide; he lunged threateningly at the strangers, who disappeared into the ruins like smoke up a chimney. "Byron, no!" May cried, but the boys had already fled: she stared after them with puzzlement, like a puppy left on the side of the road. She turned to Cecily, however, a face pinched with anger. "Now look what you did!"

"They were rude to us! They were rude about Daddy!"

"Oh, your daddy! Your daddy wouldn't care what two boys said! They were frightened!"

"I don't care – I hope they never come back! Do you hear me, stupid boys? I hope you *go away and never come back*!"

Her voice sheered off the walls of the castle, *go away, never come back*: both girls felt certain she'd been heard. May stared into the ruins forlornly, her hands fallen to her sides. A pair of larks flew by, slinging toward the river. Byron's gaze followed them. "They were just frightened," muttered May.

She swung away and stalked out from the shadows, leaving the plate where it lay. She passed her frowning hostess sporting an impressive furrow of her own. The sight of it pierced Cecily with an arrow of dismay. "Only you and I are allowed to play in the castle," she said, but the establishment of this exclusive club failed to right what had gone wrong. Distressed with herself as she so frequently was, Cecily hurried after her evacuee. She ploughed through swampy puddles, ignored the vicious spikes of thistle. They reached the gully where the river ran without exchanging a word, and gazed down at the water.

". . . Shall we ask Mama to take us into the village today? I have money."

May shrugged, refusing to be drawn. The water surged over the stepping-stones; May did not offer to carry her companion across. She forded the current like an Amazon, leaving Cecily to scramble from shore to shore with a hand on Byron for balance. Water got into her shoes and somehow into her eye. By the time she dragged herself up the far bank, Cecily was utterly crushed. "I'm sorry!" she bawled.

May flung a dismissive glance. "What are you sorry about? You weren't taken from your mother and put on a train and sent to a place you'd never been. You didn't sit on a floor and hope you were nice enough for somebody to want you. You don't have to live with strangers every day – even kind strangers are still strangers. You don't know what that's like!"

"Oh, May! Are you unhappy? Do you hate me?"

"I don't hate you," May answered, "and I'm not unhappy. But I might have to stay at Heron Hall for a long time, Cecily. Mum said it might be months and months, depending on the war. So you can't keep treating me like a guest, or like – like your best friend—"

"Don't you want to be my friend?"

"I *do*, you *are* my friend, but can't I be – someone you don't have to *take care of* all the time?"

Cecily tripped, lurched wretchedly on. She knew what May meant: she meant she did not want a shadow in the shape of Cecily. It was hurtful – Cecily believed the only thing that mattered was to be included, needed, remembered – but she struggled not to be hurt. "I'll try," she said. "I'll try to treat you more like – a brother?"

"Or a sister?"

That was a better idea, and Cecily brightened. "I don't have a sister, so I don't know how to treat one, but I'll try my best."

"I don't have a sister either," said May. Mercifully, she slowed. "I've got you, though – and you've got me. We can practise on each other."

Cecily pranced with happiness. They were nearing the woods, and once past the trees they would be able to see Heron Hall. The prospect made Cecily want to run, to speed back to that place of warmth and certainty. On this far side of the woods, things could be unpredictable. "I'm sorry," she said, and she really was. "I wish I hadn't said nasty things to those boys. I didn't think. That's what Mama always tells me: *I never think*."

May didn't disagree. She resumed a whippet's pace over the grass. "Too late to worry now. They're probably miles away. Especially if they think Mr Lockwood's going to get a gun and shoot them."

"Yes," said Cecily. "Unless they ate that breakfast you brought, in which case they're probably already dead."

A scruff of laughter escaped May, making her frown all the deeper and walk that much faster. Cecily scurried in her wake. Even as exertion drove the brothers to the back of her mind, a thought occurred to her. Their luxurious clothing had reminded her of something, and now she remembered what it was. A *pantomime*: those boys had been dressed like characters on the stage.

THE VILLAGE GOSSIP

They asked Cecily's mother to take them to the village, and Heloise agreed as she had nothing better to do. Though there seemed nothing better for Jeremy to do either, the boy assured his mother that he'd prefer to stay behind. "I can read, I can hike, I can sweep chimneys," he said; but Cecily sensed that, although he intended to do *something*, it wasn't any of these. With money in her pocket, she couldn't care what it was.

By now the sun had gathered sufficient strength to make people shed their coats, if not their vests. The fine weather had brought the villagers out into the streets. Women strolled about in no hurry to go home, their children clamped to their hips or trailing nonchalantly behind them. Boys were unloading vans and polishing windows and carting trays of groceries here and there. Rationing had cast its miserly pall over the country but the shopkeepers were doing their best to present tasty displays to the passers-by, and there was enough for everyone, provided nobody was greedy. The girls wove past the street stalls on the heels of Heloise, looking left and right, bonked on the head by baskets, reaching out for what they shouldn't touch. Lads laughed, babies cried, women haggled, shop-bells rang. It was surprising to remember that, in places around the world, the sky was not sunny or perhaps it was too sunny, the shops were closed and empty, and some people, many people, had no home left standing, no normal life left to live. In this green village, it was a lovely day.

Heloise was not interested in bread or fruit or vegetables; instead she took the girls to a dressmaker's, where the children picked through jars of buttons while Mrs Lockwood mulled over lace, and then to a tea shop, where Heloise had tea and frilly sandwiches and the girls had malted milk and lemon cake. A lady lunching at a nearby table recognized Heloise: "Mrs Lockwood!" she chimed. "I heard you'd come up to Heron Hall with the children – very wise, and not before time. Goodness, you're looking well. And is that Cecily? Cecily! How you've grown. Your curls are lovely. No school today? You can't be sick – you're enjoying that cake, aren't you? And this little blue-eyed kitten is—?"

"This is May." Heloise abhorred chit-chat, her voice had more icing than the lemon cake. "We've taken in an evacuee for the duration."

"Truly? Aren't you good. I wish I had one. I seem to be of no use to anyone, just toddling along like it's business as usual. . . Speaking of which, how is Mr Lockwood? What's his opinion of the situation in France? Any news for those of us who can only watch and hope?"

Heloise's spoon clinked her cup. "Humphrey is well."

"And his thoughts on the situation? What's to be our next move?"

Heloise said, "My husband doesn't share official secrets with myself or with tea shops."

The woman gave a laugh that sounded pressed out of her by weights. "Forgive me! Sometimes the war feels so far away, the whole thing seems a peculiar dream. Until, of course, you hear of a local boy going missing or being killed. Then it's not a peculiar dream at all. Will you be staying at Heron Hall for the duration, Mrs Lockwood?"

"Possibly," said Heloise, "possibly not."

"Oh, you must! London is so unsafe. Personally I don't know how those poor people can endure it, the blackout, the constant worry about bombs. I'd be in a perpetual state of tension, I'd think every buzz of a fly was an aeroplane come to blow the house sky-high and tear me into a thousand pieces. . ."

The girls, wide-eyed, looked at Heloise, who said, "Cecily's father is in London, as is May's mother. I'm sure they will be perfectly secure. To think otherwise is simply encouragement to the enemy."

"Encouragement to the enemy! I didn't mean it like that—"

"And yet that is how it sounds. Encouraging to our enemy."

The woman was the kind who disliked, and was disliked; Heloise was quite the same. They turned back to their tables pleased to have added one another to their collections.

After the tea shop, mother and girls strolled the streets, Cecily pointing out from window displays things she was sure May would never have seen: baby shawls crocheted from local wool, animals fashioned from horseshoe nails, handmade leather bookmarks with tassels on one end, playing cards with northern wildflowers blossoming on the reverse sides. Heloise, perched atop a high wall of boredom, told them she'd meet them in the hat shop. Cecily and May lingered in the street. They pressed their faces to the post-office window, touched their tongues to the glass. "What do you like most in the world?" asked Cecily.

May squished her nose on the window and thought. "Giraffes."

Cecily gurgled. "Not giraffes! Something you can buy!"

"You didn't say it had to be something you could buy. Anyway, you could buy a giraffe, if you were rich enough. If you were a sultan."

Cecily offered, "One of Daddy's friends has a tiger skin on the floor."

"Ugh. Tiger skins should be on tigers."

". . . Did you hear what that lady said, about London and all the people being blown to bits?"

"Hmm."

"I should tell Daddy she encouraged the enemy. He'll put her in prison. She wouldn't be so fancy then!"

"You should do it," said May.

The postmaster was suddenly at the door. "Dirty snouts off the glass!"

May sprang backward, mortified; but Cecily, sensibilities blunted by a lifetime of reprimands, merely swiped the window with the sleeve of her cardigan and sauntered away. Inspired by such *sang-froid*, May yelled over a shoulder, "You're as dirty as – as – a nappy!" although the postmaster had returned inside by then, and possibly didn't hear.

But Heloise heard, as did the milliner. "Cecily," said her mother, "that was uncouth. I didn't raise you to scream in the street like an urchin."

"It wasn't me!"

"Don't argue." Heloise glared steadfastly at a hat. "Just apologize. Cecily."

"Sorry," Cecily sighed.

"Sorry," May whispered, when Mrs Lockwood turned away.

"It's all right," said Cecily, and it *was* all right; it made something better.

Fortunately Heloise didn't like the hats, so they were able to quickly leave. Their last stop was the grocer's, where jars of boiled sweets ranged the shelves like so many stars in the sky. Cecily magnanimously divided her loot: May chose barley twists, Cecily cornered liquorice mice. "You're a little evacuee, aren't you?" said the grocer to May.

"How can you tell?" asked Cecily.

The man said, "Oh, they all have the same look," and his wife, who was leaning on the counter, said, "As if they're not awake or asleep."

The grocer smiled at May's face, which was pretty as a freesia. "Has she been any trouble? She doesn't look like trouble."

"She's no trouble at all," said Heloise loyally.

"That's just what she looks like, a good little girl."

Cecily should have heard dull clongs of pride, but instead she found herself thinking, *How silly*. To describe May as *a good little girl* was like calling a cathedral *big* or a lion *yellow*. Half the time May wasn't good at all – she was a thief of leftovers, an escapee, a hurter-of-feelings, moody and a know-all and a bossy-boots, just now she hadn't even owned up to shouting in the street – but somehow these attributes made her *better than* good. Gripping the mice, Cecily turned away, her gaze running the shelves. She wanted May to become even worse – naughtier, bolder, more clever, more devious – and Cecily wanted to become these things with her. The grocer talked on.

"It's a privilege to have them in the village, the evacuees. A privilege and an honour. Goodness though, there's some wild ones in the mix. We get them in the shop after school,

88

pushing and shoving. They're used to city ways, of course. Quick as lightning, and smart with the mouth. We have to keep an eye on them."

"Riff-raff." The grocer's wife ceased excavating sugar from under a nail and elaborated, "Bad influences. Rue the day."

"I remember—" Heloise did so with a lurch. "I remember the billeting officer at the town hall mentioning something about troublemakers."

"It's to be expected, isn't it?"

Heloise couldn't help but glance at May. "Is it?"

"Under the circumstances, I think it is. Look, they're decent mites mostly," said the grocer. "Most evacuees I've met are no better or worse than the local kids – better, when you consider what's happening to them. Surrounded by strangers, missing their families, far away from home: it's no surprise some of them aren't jumping with joy for being here. And you know how youngsters can be when things aren't going their way – stubborn, sulky, mischievous. Not doing what their hosts tell them. Mucking about, talking back. Refusing to go to school, giving the teacher lip. Running away – packing their bags and taking to the hills, some are."

"Surely not," said Heloise.

"True!" said the grocer. "There's been five or six already made a break for home. Packed their bags and disappeared in the night, trying to go back to London. They've been caught and given a good talking-to, dragged back by the ears."

"You can't have children roaming around like foxes," said his wife. "That's not what anyone agreed to."

The man waved his heavy hands. "But dragged back to *what*, is what you have to wonder. I mean, I don't think a happy child would run away from his hosts. Do *you* want to run away?" He loomed over the counter at May.

"No," said the evacuee.

"No, you don't. That's because you're happy. Landed on your feet, you have, there at Heron Hall. But not all your little friends have been so fortunate."

His wife snorted like a dubious pig in an apron. "There'd be no pleasing some of them, not if they were sent to Buckingham Palace itself."

The grocer winced. "Don't I know it. You don't own a sweets shop and not learn a thing or two about the fussiness of kids. Still, I bet there's plenty who took an evacuee just to get another pair of hands on the farm or around the house. I bet there's plenty who saw an opportunity to take their misery out on someone else's poor child."

"Hear him." The wife's eagle eye never left her crusted nails. "Always believing the worst of people."

"Sweetheart, we're in a war! If that doesn't make you believe the worst of people, what on earth will? No, my sympathies are with the children. Good luck to them, I say. You do what you've got to do. You've got to sulk, you sulk. You want to run off, you get going. You've got to stick up for yourself in this world. No one fights your battles for you."

"Listen to it." The wife rolled her eyes.

"There's something to be said for stoicism," said Heloise, who'd never had to learn it herself. "You don't simply run away from what doesn't suit you. If we all did that, well . . . who would fight the war?"

"That's sense," said the wife, and it was; so much so that the grocer pretended not to hear. But feeling generously disposed towards all children, and particularly to their representative May, before he shelved the jar of liquorice mice he invited her to extend a paw and pluck from amid the sin-black rodents a particularly bulky specimen.

The day-trippers returned to the street and walked it in silence – a silence that caused Cecily physical pain. For the entire length of the road she battled to keep the story of the brothers in Snow Castle from hissing out like air from a tyre. *Mama!* she craved to say. *I've met some runaway children, I've talked to them, they're hiding in Snow Castle, I can take you to them!* But May was marching along tight-lipped, and Cecily understood that if she ever hoped to be as bold and devious as her newfound sister – if, for that matter, she wished to remain on speaking terms with her – then the tale was not to be told. It was an agonising situation, for Cecily did relish gossip, and the brothers had been so appalling that it would be a pleasure to tell. . . Yet she also knew that she would never tell. She would keep a thousand secrets rather than lose the sister she'd gained.

May Bright was definitely a Bad Influence.

Home at Heron Hall, they found Jeremy with the day's newspapers spread out on the dining table. "Reading again!" sighed Cecily. "You read too much, Jem. There's only sad bad things in the newspapers. Horrible things."

"Unlike you, I don't want to live in a play-world and pretend the war isn't happening."

"I know it's happening." Her brother was being unfair. "I just wish it wasn't."

"Did you sweep the chimneys?" asked May.

Because the evacuee had such a charming way about her, Jeremy laughed. "No, not today. But I went out to have a look at Snow Castle. I wanted to see it up close before Uncle Peregrine tells us its history."

Cecily swung a worried glance to May, but the girl merely nodded. "What did you see?"

"I saw a plate, with the remains of breakfast on it. A raven was pecking at it, but it flew off when it saw me, carrying a piece of toast in its beak. What was a piece of toast doing out at Snow Castle, I wonder?"

May smiled. "Cecily and I went to the castle after breakfast. We wanted a close look too. We took some scraps for the birds. But we didn't see a raven, just some slugs and stones."

"I saw slugs and stones, the raven, and two red butterflies."

The girls eyed him watchfully, but Jeremy said nothing further. "I like ravens," May said finally, and gave him the liquorice mouse.

A BLEAK PROGNOSIS

The war was a sprawling, catastrophic thing, an event that would change lives, and end them; change cities, and raze them; and mar forever the story of humankind's history. Every minute, all around the world, countless decisions were shaped by the war, from when a woman swept a path to when a man pressed a button to release a bomb. One of the smallest and most insignificant of decisions was made at Heron Hall soon after the arrival of Mrs Lockwood and the children, and this was that adults and children would dine together, rather than at separate sittings. The arrangement was easier for the depleted domestic staff, but it also suited Peregrine. He could think of nothing worse than supping with his sister-in-law, just he and she. He wouldn't have been surprised to know that Heloise felt the same way. They had things in common, as smart cynical people always do, but one of the things common to them was an awkwardness around each other. Welcome, then, was the company of the children, whose chatter filled the spaces which would otherwise yawn over the dining room.

Peregrine had spoken to his brother on the telephone that afternoon, while Heloise and the girls were in town. "Did you say hello to Daddy for me?" asked an anguished Cecily.

"No," said her uncle. "But he sends his regards to you. He tells you not to talk with your mouth full and not to bother your uncle."

"Did he say anything about – what will happen next?"

Jeremy knew from his newspapers that the war continued badly for the Allies. He also knew that, no matter what his father had said, his uncle would remember the girls at the table and tailor his answer accordingly. Yet he couldn't help asking the question anyway, because frustration chewed ceaselessly at his elbow. Trapped out here in the country he was a wild beast chained, a dog of war muzzled, a worthy warrior lamed. He roamed the corridors of Heron Hall in a simmering fury of helplessness. So he asked, knowing the answer may be dilute, but craving to hear it regardless.

Peregrine looked up from his plate. Dinner that night was leek soup followed by beef, vegetables and dumplings. There was fresh bread on the table, and plenty of butter, and both Heloise and Peregrine had wine. Still to come was plum pudding and cream. One day the stingy fingers of the war might reach into the kitchen of Heron Hall, but that day wasn't today. Peregrine's glance went round the table, returned to his nephew. "France, the Netherlands and Belgium have fallen," he said. "They are occupied countries now, and largely powerless. The Germans are massing their aircraft on the coast of France, noses pointed in our direction. Their army is preparing to cross the Channel for a ground invasion. Our beaches are being strung with barbed wire, but this probably won't inconvenience the tanks for long. The outlook is poor, as you see. Some people are saying it's time to hand London over while she's still standing. Give Hitler the jewel he wants for his crown."

Although Jeremy already knew this and more, it rattled him to hear it spoken aloud by someone he trusted. It was Cecily who filled the silence. "Hand London over," she said. "You mean, surrender?"

"We can't." May spoke stonily. "If we surrender, all those soldiers who've died would be wasted. . ."

"I agree," said Jeremy. "We mustn't surrender, not ever. No matter what happens."

"Daddy won't let them win."

Cecily said it with such well-fed certainty that the conversation stopped as if at a trench. Annoyance flew across Jeremy's face; he asked, "What will happen if they do come here, Uncle?"

"They won't. Daddy will keep them out."

"Shut up, Cecily!" Her brother actually kicked the underside of the table. "Uncle? What will happen if they come here? What will happen if they win?"

He asked it with vehemency, wanting the truth from this man with whom he'd spent many of his life's happiest hours, who had always treated him with the respect due somebody older. But, "You're a boy of imagination," Peregrine replied. "What do you imagine will happen?"

Jeremy's gaze wobbled over the table and met for a moment the sapphire eyes of May which looked back steadily, steelishly. She looked ready to take up arms and confront the Führer all by herself. It was Heloise, however, who spoke. "For goodness sake, Peregrine, can we talk of something other than the war? I fail to see how turning the subject over like compost can do anything except raise its stink."

"It's important. . ."

"It's utterly drab. What will happen will happen. Discussing it at the dinner table will make no difference to our fate at all. For the moment, the war is far away. It hasn't touched any of us terribly. So let us spare ourselves while we can."

An observer, watching closely, would have seen both Jeremy and May lower their eyes in a withdrawing way, the behaviour of secret-keepers who feel themselves alone. But no one was watching closely, and, "Daddy will protect us," Cecily told herself, sotto voce.

"Very well, what shall we talk of instead?" asked Peregrine. "While the war rages across Europe, what subject fits our preference for lightness and joy?"

"Don't mock, Peregrine."

"I do not mean to."

"I think you do."

"No arguing at the table!" warned Cecily.

May looked up. "Snow Castle?" she said.

"Yes!" Cecily yiked. "The story!"

"After supper," said Peregrine, "not during it."

"What story is this?" asked Heloise.

Jeremy explained, "Uncle Peregrine is going to tell us the story of Snow Castle. It's history—"

"It's gruesome!"

"It's certainly not lightness and joy."

"—so it's not really *storytelling*, it's *teaching*, isn't it? And if Uncle Peregrine is *teaching us*, then we needn't go to school in the village, need we, Mother?"

Heloise sipped from her glass – one of many sips she'd taken so far – and considered her son with a cool eye. Perhaps she remembered the conversation in the grocery shop, the mention of riff-raff and unruliness in the village classrooms. Heloise Lockwood had invested in the slight frame of her boy all her hopes and ambitions; but Jeremy had reached a difficult age, and his mother's dreams could easily become unstuck by months spent in a small room under the influence of malcontents. Nevertheless Heloise was not

97

the type to give in easily: "I suppose it's education of a sort – for now. Not for ever."

The children hunched gleefully into themselves. "After supper," Peregrine promised.

But, as is usual when children are longing for an adult to fulfil a promise, there was a drag of endless time to be fidgeted through before the obligation was met. The main course had to be finished, some digestion must be done, and dessert needed to be consumed as painstakingly as a last meal. The children were then sent off to Peregrine's study, which was progress of a sort; but here, far from the dining room, they could not exert the pressure of their excitement, and had to sit among the rock samples and carriage clocks in a torment of impatience. The wine bottle must be drained, a subject brought to a close, the table vacated, the washroom visited. When Peregrine finally limped into the study, followed by Byron and eventually by his sister-in-law, he found three children quite bad-tempered with waiting; yet he made them wait further while the fire was stoked, the armchair repositioned, claret poured, a thin cigar lit. Heloise curled up close to the flames, Cecily and May lay on rugs beside Byron, and Jeremy sat on the floor with his back to his mother, near enough for her to occasionally reach out and stroke his glossy hair.

"You have been warned," Peregrine began. "This story is not a pleasant one. In some ways it is like the fairytales of old, when fairies had a taste for the macabre. But it is not a fairytale: this story is true, and you can look up the facts in history books; and when the truth has been lost in secrecy the gaps are filled by rumours which may have been true, or may have been wishful thinking, or may have been barefaced lies. It's a story you might think couldn't happen now, when we have cars and telegrams and all kinds of modern ways. You might think it's a story from a dark age. But the world is at war as we sit here, tearing itself up like a pack of wolves: maybe, hundreds of years from now, this era we live in will likewise appear a dark and ignorant age. At the end of the story you might find yourself judging some of its characters harshly, but always remember that the world was very different then – yet also, underneath, much the same."

Cecily, not sure she followed all of what her uncle had said, glanced at her companions. May was cradling Byron's paw, her face pinkened by the fire. She would understand everything – the bizarre thought came to Cecily that May already knew the story they were about to hear, that perhaps she was even *in* it. Cecily looked at the girl's stockinged legs, her starfish hands, the bow in her hair that was falling loose; and was engulfed by a desire to protect her, as well as a wish to lock her and her elfy cleverness in a cupboard out of sight.

"Very well," said Peregrine, reaching for his glass: "let it begin."

FROM BOY TO DUKE

"The boy was born into a time of mud and splendour. In most of the world people lived hard and simple lives, farming the land or sweating in occupations by which the worker came to be known – tanner, potter, cooper, wheeler – as if the work was more important than the person who did it. This was the world of hovels and shovels, dirt roads, fields and forests: a time of mud.

"It was not the world the boy knew. For him, it was a time of splendour. The youngest son of aristocrats, he knew thick blankets, rich food, fine clothes. He knew servants and horses, feasts and learning, etiquette and tournaments. All this luxury, however, did not bring with it contentment. His was a family which believed itself born to rule. Distantly related to royalty, they naturally wanted to be royal. And to become a family of kings, they needed to remove from their path all others who would claim the crown.

"The work was bloody: in the battles which accompanied his family's rise, the boy saw his father and eldest brother killed. These losses only increased the family's determination. Gathering their supporters, they destroyed the royal army and forced the King, a weak sick man, off the throne. The boy's oldest surviving brother proclaimed himself regent, and suddenly the boy was no longer merely a child: brother to a king, he was now royal, and we shall call him Duke, which was one of many names he would come to have during his life, and beyond it.

"At this time the Duke was nine years old. He had lost a father and a brother; but he had two surviving brothers, one of whom had stolen by force the ultimate power in the land. The Duke had learned, from this, a lesson he would not forget: *might crushes right*. We'll leave him, for the time being, to think about this in private while he grows a little older.

"The Duke's brother, the new king, was loved by the people from the start. He was youthful in a time of decrepitude, tall in an age of stubbiness, comely in a time of ugliness, lavish in this era of mud. All the world's prettiest princesses vied for his attention. Eventually he chose a wife, but she was not one of those regal ladies. She was, in fact, a commoner. The princesses were appalled, as were the people. Our little Duke did not like the new queen, and it's true that, in all sorts of ways, the King could have done better. The girl was vain, greedy, ambitious. But she was beautiful and the King believed he loved her, and while in that hard world love did not count for much, in this case it had the power to turn a commoner into a queen.

"Power: I want you to remember this word. I want you to say it to yourself, feel its weight in your hand. Look into its dark depths every time this story takes a turn."

"Power," whispered May.

"Power," affirmed Cecily. Jeremy glanced testily at the girls; Peregrine poured more claret.

"Time passed, and three princesses were born – the youngest of whom, I'm happy to say, was named Cecily – and the King was delighted with each. He was especially pleased, however, when the Queen produced a son. They christened the child *Edward*, and the King and his country rejoiced. Finally here was an heir. The King, however, had no time to celebrate. His brother – not our Duke, but the middle brother, Clarence – had taken into his head the idea that he, not his brother, should be king. He made a fuss, embarrassed the King, dug out the outcast king and tried to sit him back on the throne. The King forgave his lunatic sibling and slung the old king back in prison; but his rivals had been stirred now, and he was forced to fight again for his realm. Many pretenders to the throne were slain on the field. Eventually triumphant, the King returned home to cheers. The merchants loved him, the women loved him, it seemed the Heavens above loved him too.

"At the King's side marched his brother, our Duke – a faithful brother, although no longer little. He was now a young man of eighteen. Unlike his brawny brother the King, the Duke was small and lightly built, dark-haired and blue-eyed. Years later, when the Duke was long dead, rumours spread that he'd been physically warped, a goblin; but portraits painted while he lived showed a man shaped as any other, and certainly he was as fit and feisty as are most young men. He liked to hawk and hunt, to drink and eat, to brawl and sleep. He liked having money, and spending it. He liked to make people laugh, and to show off his wit and education. He wanted to be popular and have friends. He wanted, in summary, to find a good place for himself in the world.

"But while he was, in many ways, a man like all others, our Duke was not the same as they were. His entire life had been shaped by bloodshed. He had fought on battlefields, and he had killed. He'd learned lessons from his clever brother, the King, and from his blockhead brother, Clarence. He'd learned to be valorous, cunning, and quiet; reliable, daring, and thoughtful. He'd learned, in short, what it takes to succeed. The King trusted him, and rewarded him with titles that decorated our cat-like Duke like so much overwrought jewellery.

"So now, at last, the battles had been fought, a strong king had been crowned, an heir had been born, and peace could reign. There was one final task to attend to, however, and for its fulfilment the King turned to his trustworthy brother. In the depths of night, the Duke visited the old king in his cell. The next morning the old man was found with blood flowing from him, the brains wrung out of his skull."

"Hawg!" crowed Cecily.

"Peregrine!" scolded Heloise.

The storyteller was unrepentant. "It's vital you understand who he was, this Duke. A creature of his upbringing and his era. A man obedient to the demands of his time. Aren't we the same?"

"I think not. One can choose what one will and will not do."

"That's true, although possibly not always true. As we speak, there are soldiers in France doing what they might not choose to do. But we mustn't judge our Duke as we would judge a man alive today. He was the product of an age of great violence. He was hardened to it, as were the people who surrounded him. Remember that – and remember the other thing."

"Power?" said Jeremy.

"Power," confirmed Peregrine. "For the person without power, there was only the mud."

"Tell us about little Cecily," begged Cecily.

"The little princess Cecily? She is growing older and more pleasing, as are all the King's children. Indeed, another prince has been born by now, making a fine pair of brothers. We'll talk about those boys later: but the Princess Cecily, I'm sorry to say, is not, and never will be, our concern."

"Aw," said Cecily.

Peregrine topped up his glass, and bolstered Heloise's too. He rang for the maid and ordered warm milk for the children. This was brought, in steaming mugs; Cecily let hers grow a crinkle of skin, fished it out and fed it to Byron.

"And so back to the Duke," Peregrine resumed. "He decided it was time to marry, and why not? Unlike the King, he wasn't so foolish as to marry for love. Love could be found anywhere, if you were a duke. But there was a young lady suitable for marrying, and she suited because she brought with her the promise of a rich estate. Land, titles—"

"Power," said Jeremy.

Peregrine smiled. "Now you understand. The Duke married into vast tracts of cool northern land with its marshes and moors, its valleys and rivers. And the people of this region, who, like their countryside, were often sneered-at as being brutish and untamed, would come to love their Duke, and claim him, and offer him a place of safety, just as he would always love and need this northern land, and the affection of its people. The couple made their home in a castle on the banks of a river in the heart of this country—"

"Snow Castle?" asked Cecily.

"– not Snow Castle – and soon they had their own little son. You might think peace should now reign: but the quest for power is strange in that, once the quest has begun, the destination always seems to shift ever further away. What power one has is never enough; whatever happiness one had turns to bitterness.

"The middle brother, Clarence, sat in his castle and stewed. After his rabble-rousing of some years earlier, the King had kept him on a short but generous leash. He had wealth and titles, yet he believed himself deprived. He wanted glory, he wanted attention, he wanted, he wanted . . . he wanted the weight of the crown. The worm that is power ate at him, stripping off his skin and lapping his blood and then gnawing at his bones. He felt unappreciated, neglected, deprived. Now the worm crawled up his spine and began to dine on his brain—"

"For goodness sake, Peregrine!"

But the children were enchanted by the machinations of this invertebrate, and tamped down Heloise's protests with waving hands. Nevertheless Peregrine abandoned the creature and sipped his claret, smiling quietly. "You can see where this is going, can't you? Demented Clarence, squawking in his castle, provoking the King and Queen's displeasure with a string of complaints and lies. Poor Clarence is digging his own grave. At last he found himself standing at the crumbly edge of it: the King had him arrested and brought before a court. The court was told of Clarence's malice and gossip, his lack of loyalty to his king. No one spoke in protest when the death sentence was pronounced – certainly not the Queen, who saw Clarence as a threat and wanted him removed. Our own Duke likewise made no attempt to save his brother. Perhaps his silence was due to powerlessness – mad Clarence was beyond redemption – or perhaps it was due to power:

the Duke would, after all, inherit the lion's share of his brother's legacy. So Clarence was put to death, and—"

"How?"

Peregrine's black glance shifted to his nephew. "I beg your pardon?"

"How did Clarence die? You told us the story was gruesome, so how did he die? Was his head chopped off? Was he pulled to pieces by horses?"

"Enough of this!" Heloise clapped her hands. "It's a dreadful story, Peregrine. Everyone murdering everyone: you'll turn the children into thugs!"

Peregrine switched his gaze to her. "We sent hundreds of men to France today. Many of them will be shot down or blown up, or captured and tortured or drowned."

"I don't want to hear about *that*, either."

"Why not? It will happen for your sake, and mine, and the children's. Therefore we *should* hear about it, shouldn't we?"

Heloise's mouth went razor-thin. "The subject of death," she said, "should not be given to children to play with as a toy. Maybe that's the reason we're in this terrible war: because boys treat death as if it's just a game."

Jeremy hit the floor with a fist, jolting Byron from his doze. "You're spoiling it, Mother! If you don't want to hear the story, you should go to bed!"

"Jeremy!"

"If you won't let Uncle Peregrine tell me the truth, I'll read it in a book!"

"Jem, be quiet! *You're* spoiling it!"

Peregrine held up a hand, calming his upset audience. "Shh. Your mother is right, Jem. How Clarence died is not important. He died, and power claimed another soul. The King built a fine tomb for him, which suggests that, for all Clarence's foolishness, the King was sorry to see him go. The Duke, for his part, blamed the Queen for his brother's downfall, and hated her even more. He retreated to the countryside, far from the royal court and its jealousies. In the deep green dales of the north, he was well-known and admired. He had friends here who would side with him if the taking of sides was needed. With the removal of Clarence the Duke had become, after the King's sons, next in line for the crown; in some quarters of the north, the King's indulgence had made the Duke more powerful than the King himself. For the Duke, a man groomed from the cradle to rise in the world, it must have been an interesting position to hold, so strong, so near to the throne. But for now he watched and waited, read his books, said his prayers.

"And what he watched was the King growing fatter."

"Yah!" laughed Cecily.

"The King in his youth had been a majestic specimen, tall, broad, hale. But by the time he was forty – an age that is elderly only to children – the years of extravagance had taken their toll. The King was as fat as a barrel, as lazy as a swine, as breathless as a cod. He was a burping, farting, flabby disgrace to behold. He'd become too lazy to think for himself, and was bossed about by his wife and her relatives. He'd handed the upbringing of his heir, little Edward, into the care of his wife's family – a family our Duke detested, don't forget; and the feeling was certainly mutual.

"And this was how everything stood – the Duke brooding, the Queen presiding – when the King went out for an afternoon's boating and came home with a chill that first laid him low, and then laid him lower. On his deathbed he commanded all enemies be friends, so the enemies shook hands and smiled. When he died, the King might have believed he was leaving behind a kingdom in tranquillity . . . but in actuality, glaring at each other across the King's corpse were two mighty rivals whose hatreds could not be healed with the shaking of hands. The Queen stood with her supporters, the Duke stood with his. And between them was a child, Prince Edward, just twelve years old. By birth he was destined to wear his father's crown – but what is destiny? Only something we think should happen, until it does not."

Peregrine had been smoking a cigar; now he pressed its stub into an ashtray and the audience watched as a last grey quiff of smoke curled into itself like a spider and died. "That's enough for tonight." Peregrine looked tired. "There's more to tell, but that's enough for now."

HOW TO PASS A RAINY
MORNING

The next morning brought something marvellous: a letter for May. So excited was Cecily by the advent of the envelope that her hand actually reached out to grab it, managing to restrain itself only at the last instant and clonking like dead wood to the table. May gazed at her name written above the address of Heron Hall. "It's from my mother," she said.

"You see!" said Cecily. "I told you she wouldn't have forgotten you. Open it!"

"She might not want to open it."

"Why not? I want to know what it says—"

"Maybe she would rather not tell you what it says," Jeremy sighed. "A letter is a private thing, Cecily."

May looked from the siblings to their uncle. He met her eye for just a moment before returning his attention to his plate. "I think," he said, "a letter should always be read in private before being inflicted on an audience, lest it be boring – or too exciting for the listeners' own good."

"I don't think May's mum would write anything *exciting*," Cecily scoffed. "She isn't a *spy* or something. She's just a housewife. There's nothing exciting about bringing in the washing."

"She was going to get a job," said May. "That's why she had to send me here."

"That's not true! She sent you here in case of an air raid. She didn't want a bomb dropping on your head."

A frown came to May's small face. "It is true. She isn't afraid of bombs. She was getting a job to help us win the war."

"Haw! What job could your mum do, to help win the war? She couldn't do something proper, like Daddy does."

The frown grew deeper. "She was going to work in a factory where they make aeroplanes, or be a bus conductor or an ambulance driver, something like that."

"A bus conductor!" It was killingly funny. "As if conducting a bus could win the war!"

"It's better than doing *nothing*," said the evacuee.

If anyone thought of Heloise lounging upstairs in her bed with a long day of nothingness stretching before her, nobody mentioned it. Jeremy looked to the window, sunk in heavy silence. The carving of Peregrine's breakfast seemed to require concentration. "Read it to yourself, May, in your room," he said. "Be quiet and eat your breakfast, Cecily."

Cecily shuffled like a pony that's being prevented from charging off where it will; she consoled herself by observing, "It's a very flat envelope. I don't think there's a present inside." And that at least was something to be satisfied about.

The sunshine of the previous day had gone and the sky was low and sour, the same dire colour as the newspapers that shouldered for space between the plates. Cecily said, "Tell us more about the Duke, Uncle Peregrine," but her uncle said, "No. The Duke's story is for telling in the night." When the evacuee, having finished her breakfast, asked for permission to leave the table, Cecily jack-in-a-boxed out of her chair. But, "Sit down," said Peregrine, in such a tone that a whole herd of Cecilys would have resumed their seats. "May, you may leave the table. Cecily, stay. I have a matter to discuss with you."

"But—"

He pointed a talon at her chair; his niece plumped down into it. Glumly she watched May disappear out the door; turning to her captor she asked wearily, "What is it, Uncle?"

"It's rats."

"Rats?" Cecily blanched. If she knew anything, she knew she didn't like rats.

"Cook believes there are rats in the larder. If not rats, mice. If not mice, weevils. If not weevils, children."

"Hmm," said Cecily.

"To say *children* is unfair. One child. One rack of biscuits, and one child."

Jeremy, reading the newspaper but listening, shook his head in disgust.

"Maybe it was a rat?" suggested Cecily.

Her uncle wouldn't be swayed. "A female child with blond ringlets and a pot belly, who shares in common with the rat only that creature's legendary sneakiness."

Cecily always knew when she was beaten. She had no belief in going down fighting, but surrendered the moment it seemed her youth would be the best defence. "They were so delicious," she said, and let the memory of the biscuits play upon her face to prove how helpless she had been before them. "What's my punishment?"

Peregrine looked at Jeremy, who folded back the newspaper and turned it to his sister. "The crossword."

Cecily screamed. "That's not fair!"

"The crossword it is!" Peregrine passed sentence: "Miss Cecily Lockwood cannot leave this room until the crossword is done. What's the first clue, Jem?"

"The queenly state of Australia. Eight letters."

Cecily clutched her head.

With the help of her brother and uncle the puzzle was complete in an hour, but the process sapped Cecily's joy in being alive. She left the breakfast room feeling dazed, plodded up the stairs. She'd forgotten about May, but the

113

fact of the evacuee's existence returned to her on the landing. She found the girl in her bedroom, curled up on her pillows and reading a book. Cecily reeled in, slumped against the bedpost, puddled to the floor. "Are you hurt?" May asked.

"My brain is."

May tucked the book under a pillow. "Look at the rain," she said, and Cecily hoisted her head high enough to see across the quilt and out the window to where rain was falling in workmanlike fashion, as if obliged to do so; perhaps it was.

". . .Did you read your mother's letter?"

"Mmm."

"Did she send you anything besides the letter? A postcard or a ribbon, something like that?"

"No," said May, "just a letter."

"Ah." Cecily found she had lost much interest in Mrs Bright's epistle. "Is she well?"

"Yes, she's well."

"I hope my daddy is well."

Again the girls looked to the weeping sky. The ruts in the land would be filling up and overflowing. "I wonder about those two boys," murmured Cecily.

"Maybe they've gone home."

"Do you think so? To which home? Back to where they were billeted? Or home to London?"

"I don't know." May watched the rain. "It was hard to understand those boys."

"I didn't like those boys, but I felt sorry for them. Didn't you?"

"Sort of," said May.

"I felt – *strange* about them. Like they were our dreadful enemies, but also that they couldn't hurt us. They were scary, but I wasn't frightened of them. They made me cross, but I also felt sad for them. I didn't want to talk to them, but I just couldn't stop talking. . ."

Cecily halted, pressed her face into the quilt. She hadn't known she'd had these entangled feelings about the boys. It made her feel peculiar, as if her mind had gone off somewhere without her. She vowed not to think about them any more. The shock of the crossword was wearing away and she felt revived enough to say, "We can't go outside in this weather. Shall we play hide-and-seek?"

"Yes," said May.

They complicated the traditional rules of the game by bringing Byron into it: for much of the morning the girls and the dog played an indoor version of fox-hunting, the hiding child being the fox, the seeking child and the Newfoundland playing the huntress and her hound. Through the cavernous rooms of Heron Hall the fox scurried, burying herself within cupboards, behind curtains, inside mighty chests. With methodical determination the hound and huntress followed, snuffling under tables, investigating stairwells, peering behind doors. The third floor of the house, where the staff had their rooms, was off-limits, as were the private rooms of Heloise and Peregrine; still there remained countless nooks in which a child-fox could hide. Nonetheless it was a surprisingly nerve-racking game for the fox, who dodged and weaved and doubled-back yet was gradually but relentlessly cornered by the hound. When May, the huntress, hauled aside a basket of bones to unearth her quarry from beneath a table in the library, she found Cecily rolled into a chunky ball with tears coursing down her face. "What's the matter?" she asked.

"I miss my daddy!"

May was accustomed to Cecily's daddy appearing in conversation at the slightest of invitations, but this time his arrival surprised even her. "Why? Are you scared?"

"No, it's only – you know how you always go to museums with your dad? Well, I always play hide-and-seek with my dad. It would make you cry if you went to a museum without your dad, wouldn't it? Well, hide-and-seek is making me cry. . ."

May blinked several times. "My dad –" she began, and stopped. She said, "We won't play if you don't want to."

Cecily unrolled from below the table, grabbed Byron and wiped her face on him. "I'm not really crying," she sighed. "I just miss Daddy. I worry about him. He has a very serious job. He must get tired. He's alone. Do you think he'll be all right?"

"Probably. I think so."

"Why do you think so?"

"Well. . . He sounds like the kind of person who is always all right."

"Is he? I suppose he is." Cecily mopped her eyes and smiled. "Shall we keep playing?"

"I don't mind."

But they didn't keep playing; the library was a fascinating place, with shelves stacked with tomes of all hues and heft laddering up to a domed ceiling where a skylight let in a shaft of the muffled day. The girls moved like moths from shelf to shelf, alighting here and there to draw a book from between its fellows. Many of the books were old, and puffed out clouds of elderly breath when they were opened. The odour, waved away, revealed words written on rice-paper, in foreign languages, in words understandable yet incomprehensible, occasionally no words at all. Some books had pictures, many painted straight on to the page. There were mountains, exotic birds, literary villains. "Ugh," May grimaced, and Cecily hurried to see: a book full of drawings of naked men and naked women in graceful poses. The girls stared, turned the pages in silence. The various lumps and bumps seemed nothing to do with them; but, aware they were making landmark discoveries, their cheeks reddened, they flinched in dismay. "Put it away," Cecily whispered, and May shelved the book promptly, as if it were poison; only then did they giggle delightedly. They ran to the window and refreshed themselves looking out on to flowerbeds and tumbling rain. "I love this house!" said May, the declaration bursting free.

"Yargh!" trumpeted Cecily, who could summon no other means to describe her satisfaction. "It's not like your house, is it?"

The child gave a rollicking laugh. "My house is just a matchbox!"

"With only one match left inside!"

"Huh?" said May.

"*You're* gone, and your *dad* is gone, and only your mum is left! I hope she doesn't get burned!"

It was supposed to be light-hearted but, as usual with Cecily, something went askew and it came out rather wrong. "She won't," the poor girl added.

May only smiled, and pushed away from the window. The library's fireplace was enclosed in carved black marble. On the mantelpiece, in a silver frame, was a photograph of a woman. She was a pretty lady in a long dress, sitting on a low wall with a hat hanging loose in her hands. She was smiling in a way that suggested she couldn't blame the camera for wanting to take a picture of her. "That's her." Cecily was reverent. "Uncle Peregrine's wife. She died when she had a baby. Then the baby died. They both died. So sad."

May, chin tipped, studied the photograph. "Do you think he remembers her?"

"Of course he does! He loved her. You don't forget people you love. Maybe you forget their faces, but you don't forget the love." This sounded grand but was in fact entirely speculation; no one Cecily loved had ever died; she hustled

118

May's attention away. Confettied on the hearth were leftovers of papers which had been fed to the fire, and the girls picked up the remnants carefully and put them into the grate. On some of the scraps could be seen handwriting, ragged words which made no sense: *never we—*, *the governm—*, *most urgen—*, *I once mor—*. Beside the fireplace stood a trim table with legs like fine flutes; on its surface were spread antique drawings of skeletons both animal and human. May wiped her hands on her cardigan before she touched the pages. "What a lot of bones a snake has."

Cecily looked. "Like a fallen-down sock."

The flensed creature stared through white holes where its eyes would have been. It seemed to be asking something. It seemed to want something from them. A promise to do a thing it itself could no longer do.

"I don't think you should play in here." Jeremy spoke from the doorway, startling the girls. "You'll destroy something. Everything is precious."

"We're not playing, we're looking."

The boy's gaze shifted to the basket of bones. "Watch Byron doesn't eat those. Some of them might be dinosaur bones."

Cecily rolled her eyes. "By-By wouldn't eat a stinky old *dinosaur.*"

"These drawings are beautiful," said May.

Jeremy accepted the compliment as if he'd done the illustrations himself. He came into the room, picked through

119

the bones, and showed the girls how a real horse vertebra compared with the pen-and-ink image of one; both were like the pieces of a clunky puzzle. "I want to be an archaeologist when I'm older," he told May. "I'll need to know about anatomy and geology. Mother and Fa don't approve, but it's what I want to do."

"If it's what you want to do, you should do it."

The boy smiled ruefully. "That's easy to say. It's not that simple. Sometimes I think I have no right to live inside my skin." He ran a meditative hand over Byron's head, said, "I bet your father wouldn't mind if you wanted to become an archaeologist, would he?"

"I don't think so," said May.

"No. He'd be proud that you wanted to do something interesting, not just do what he has done. . . Any news of him in your mother's letter?"

May shook her head. "No."

"And has your mum found work?"

"*A letter is a private thing*, Jem!"

"She has a job sewing parachutes," said May.

"Parachutes?" Cecily gagged. "Parachutes! How silly!"

Her brother wheeled, fixing on his sister a glare that would have crippled a more sensitive soul. "You're so ignorant, Cecily! What's silly about it? If your plane was shot down and you had to bail out, you wouldn't think it was silly. If you were falling towards the ground at a hundred miles an hour, you wouldn't think it was silly. You'd think May's mother was the cleverest person who'd ever lived! There'd be only one person who mattered in the whole world, and that would be May's mum!"

"It just sounds funny." Cecily snuffled. "*Parachutes.*"

Jeremy looked as if a shard of metal was working its way into his heart. Stricken, furious, to drive it deeper he asked, "So she's working in a factory, May?"

"In a factory, with other ladies."

"That's happening a lot now, isn't it – ladies doing the work men used to do. Factories, mining, engineering, farming. . . They're at the front as well. Nursing, and manning radios. Resistance fighting too, I've read."

"*Ladies*," said Cecily. "Ladies, Jem. Not fourteen-year-old boys. Fourteen-year-old boys have to go to the country with their mummies."

A lesser young man might have struck his sister for her cruelty, but Jeremy only turned his face away. He looked at the vertebra in his hand, closed his fingers around its strong white shape; released it, and placed it on top of the sheaf of drawings. "Be careful what you touch," he said quietly. "Nothing in here belongs to you." And walked out of the room.

Peregrine was not at the table for lunch, which wasn't unusual as he was often busy outside the house or in his study. At the start of the meal, and again near its end, they heard the telephone ring. Footsteps went up and down the staircase, and Hobbs brought the car to the front of

121

the house. None of this was particularly odd, but Jeremy asked, "What's going on?"

"Is something going on?" said Heloise. "I have no idea."

The boy stared at her as children will when they know that a parent who is capable of lying is actually doing so. But Heloise was polished in everything she did, and her son saw nothing, when he looked at her, but his own eyes staring glassily back at him.

"It's stopped raining," Cecily observed. "Can we play outside this afternoon?"

It wasn't necessary to beg permission, as Heloise never minded where the children played, so long as it was out of earshot. On their way to collect their coats the girls passed Jeremy hovering in the hallway where he could scope out the great staircase and the front door. "Come outside and play," invited May, and gave him a dose of her sparkling eyes and winning smile; and Jeremy mumbled, "No, you go, I have to. . ." and trailed off, his sights returning to the stairs. So May and Cecily put on their wellingtons and went out into the day without him: "The trouble with Jem," his sister opined, "is that he's like a guard dog who forgets he's also just a dog." And given that Cecily was like a cat whose sole desire was to curl up on somebody's lap and sleep, May supposed her opinion an educated one.

THE CASTLE SPEAKS

Because the earth was soaked and the air so cool, they played in the snug shelter of the outbuildings. The stable walls were hung with old harnesses which rattled musically, and the mangers were dusted with chaff that smelt good. Inside large bins with flat metal lids were troves of grain into which the girls plunged their arms to the elbows. Hunks of wood were piled in the lumber-house, packed into every corner and stacked up to the roof, waiting their turn for the fire. The sight of the severed limbs lumped one upon the other, their very deadness and splintered silence made Cecily sigh, "Poor trees."

They explored the knife-house and the kennels, places they'd investigated countless times already; nothing had changed. They clumped about on the cobbles, leaping heavily in their boots. They took turns hanging on the gate and being propelled through the deep arc of its swing. Byron became bored, and slouched back to the house. Finally the girls grew still.

"What shall we do?"

"We shall. . . We shall. . . We shall go to the henhouse?"

"Cook got angry last time we did that. She said we made the hens go off the lay. Besides, I don't like those birds. They've got mean eyes."

May propped her chin on the rail. "We shall . . . go to the lake? There's frogs."

"Urgh, frogs!"

". . . I wish there was a pony."

"There used to be a black Shetland called Jezebel, when I was little. She's dead now. She bit me. Ponies aren't as nice as you think."

"What will we do then?"

"I don't know." There was nothing. There was only one thing. They both knew it must be done. May slipped from the gate.

Although the puddles were wider and the land soaked, the long walk across the woods and fields to the ruins did not seem, to Cecily, as arduous as it had the day before, when they'd taken the breakfast leftovers to the castle. Part of Cecily hesitated to return, remembering the horridness of the boys and her own horridness in reply, as well as the painful conversation with May which had followed. But Cecily was not the type to dwell, and all this already seemed the happenings of long ago, the painful edges dulled. She was buoyed by a sense of ownership, compelled by the need to be included, and driven by curiosity: she could not believe the brothers would still be lurking about the miserable ruins, but if they were – well, that was endurance worth witnessing first-hand.

The rain had made the river faster but hardly deeper, and the girls gripped each other's wrists and helped one another cross. They flinched to feel the water against their wellies, chortled when their boots slithered on the slick embankment and felled them to their hands and knees. But as they approached the ruins they grew subdued, and stepping through the cold still air Cecily had the thought that no one had ever laughed in this place – that throughout the long unspooling of the centuries the stones and their surrounding trees had never heard such a thing. Snow Castle had been built in silence to hold silence, and silently it had dropped in pieces to the ground. "I wish we'd brought Byron," she whispered, and her words came out in fog that floated, as if captured and pondered, and then, as if dismissed, disappeared.

May looked around at the remains of the castle. The jagged walls dripped water and oozed slime. Moss grew between the stones, and grey mould smudged them. Spiderwebs, lit by raindrops, sagged in every angle. Grass grew up the walls, long threads reaching for the sunlight; over the toppled stone it grovelled messily, without aim. As she walked into the ghostly core of the ruins, water smattered her to the elbows. "Hello?" she called.

Hello, the castle replied.

A flock of birds took flight somewhere; Cecily did not see and hardly heard them, but she felt it, their urgent flying away. The castle towered above the children, so little of itself remaining, yet so completely *present* – as if it had never needed ceilings and roofs and floors, this tattered wreckage being sufficient and even what it preferred. Cecily found herself scanning the highest reaches, where the raw edges of stone met the meek sky, not knowing what she expected to see up there but knowing she wouldn't be surprised to see it, either – a watching eye, a reaching arm, a body encased in stone for centuries yet still faintly alive. With a shiver she bumped her gaze to earth, to the shelf where May had left the breakfast plate. The plate was gone, presumably returned to the kitchen by Jeremy; but the ground beneath the shelf showed a scattering of crumbs. Not the crumbs left by children or even by fairytale children, but crumbs thrown about by the investigations of birds.

"Hello?" May called, louder this time.

The castle growled back, *Hello*.

"Is anybody here?"

The castle wondered, *Here? Anybody?*

"They're not here." Cecily's heart was making its presence felt, knocking as if it wanted to tell her something.

"Hello, are you here? You two boys?"

Two boys here, two boys?

They waited while the echo had its amusement, gambolling from wall to wall like a nasty clown. May placed a hand on a shoulder of stone, then snatched it back as though the marble burned. "They must have gone."

"The rain drove them off," Cecily agreed – quietly, so the castle wouldn't hear. And both girls thought of rain not as being wet and cold and to be avoided whenever possible, but rather as being talismanic, as if rain were related to garlic, and this was a place of vampires. May looked at the remains, the stumps of beams, the deep fireplaces, the arching gaps through which someone must have once surveyed the land. The ground around the walls had been dented into bowls by centuries of dripping water. In corners of stone hung clouds of fog like watchful forest animals, wary but also willing to attack. "I'm glad," Cecily whispered. "I'm glad they've gone." And it wasn't the horridness of the brothers that made her glad, but because she didn't wish to know anyone who could find these lonesome ruins a satisfactory place to be.

May frowned. She was not quite ready to walk away. "Hello!" she hollered. "Is somebody here?"

You will never leave this place, replied Snow Castle.

At least that was what it seemed to say; Cecily whimpered, "May, let's go. I'm cold. I don't feel well. There's no one here."

"All right," conceded May. But as they walked away she kept glancing back, unconvinced.

Returning to Heron Hall, the girls discovered they had missed a scene: Heloise was in her bedroom nursing upset feelings, Jeremy was in his own room fuming, and the household was stepping on tiptoe, leery of disturbing either of them. The housekeeper, Mrs Winter, was having tea in the kitchen with Cook; Cecily and May sidled into fuggy gaps around the stove, accepted tea and sultana biscuits, and prised from these two stone-faced women a little blood-warming gossip. While the girls had been playing in the outbuildings, oblivious to the whole world, Peregrine had come down with his overnight case, dealing commands to his staff as he went, clearly intending to depart the Hall and to do so in some hurry – Hobbs had the car running, the front door was already open. It was at the door that Peregrine had met Jeremy, the boy "spiky as the labrador who ate the hedgehog," according to Mrs Winter. "Not a clue what was happening, but still he wanted a piece of it. Mr Lockwood could have been off to keep an appointment with a Turkish firing-squad for all the lad knew, but still he wants to follow him about like a mutt."

Cecily paused in the work of shovelling biscuit into her mouth to explain, "He wants to be where the action is."

"Action! Your mother gave him action. *Jeremy*! she says. *I've just about had it with you!*"

"Ooh." It was rare for Heloise to lose her temper with her favourite: Cecily was thrilled. "Mama was there too?"

"She came into the hall at the same time as Mr Lockwood came downstairs, just in time to hear your brother plead *Uncle, take me with you.* As if he's a setter and Mr Lockwood's going duck-shooting. Mr Lockwood looks at him and says *Jem, you know I can't.* And Mrs Lockwood says *Jeremy, how many times must you be told? Until I am blue in the face? London is not safe! You are staying here, and you are not leaving!* The lad starts whining, but your mother talks over him. *I won't have you arguing and resisting every moment of every day! Don't you think I have enough worries? I'm amazed you can be so selfish!'*

Cecily was enjoying everything about this: the warmth of the stove, the sweetness of the tea, the meatiness of the gossip and, especially, the housekeeper's impersonation of her mother. She reached for another biscuit, the very largest; tractored it in.

"To which the lad starts dancing up and down in a devil of a fuss. *Mother!* he screams – really screams, like a wounded rabbit. *I'll be safe with Uncle Peregrine, I'll be safe with Father! Why can't I go?* And Mrs Lockwood shrieks *Because you're a child! You're a hindrance, not a help! Do you think this is a game, Jeremy? That your father and uncle can leave aside the small matter of the war to attend the needs of a child?"*

Several crumbs popped out of Cecily: "Ho ho! Jem doesn't like it when people call him a child."

"Apparently!" said Mrs Winter. "He didn't care for it at all. *I'm not a child!* he bellows. *If I had to, I could kill a man!"*

Cecily hooted; Cook shook her head. "Can you imagine!" The housekeeper couldn't help grinning. "He's springing about like a flea-bit yorkie, howling about killing people. You can guess how it went down with Mrs Lockwood – I thought she was going to be the lad's first victim. Just roll over dead with her arms and legs in the air."

Cecily rocked in her chair at the picture, hands clamped to her face; but Cook said dourly, "You can laugh, little lady, but it's a terrible thing. A sweet boy talking about killing people. Quite ready to step up and kill people. That's what this war's done."

"Jem couldn't kill a butterfly!"

"But that's the thing, see? A boy who can't kill a butterfly wants to kill a man. Where's the good in that? Where's the victory in that?"

Cecily didn't even try to understand what the woman was talking about, but reached instead for a biscuit. Mrs Winter slid the plate across the stove. "No more, pet, you'll spoil your dinner."

"What was Mr Lockwood doing?" asked May.

"Well, staring at mother and son in amazement! Probably wondering why he let such wild beasts take up residence in his house. *You think I'm weak and stupid!* says the lad, and his mother, who's like a hissing cat, says *What I think you are is infantile, and I've had enough of it! I'm fed up with the moroseness, the martyrdom. If you don't improve your behaviour, I shall send you abroad.*"

"Oh!" *Abroad* was a bit serious, this conflict was getting out of hand. "What did Jem say?"

"It pulled him up on his rope, that's certain. Threatening him with banishment, that's what his mother was doing, simply because she knew it would break his heart. That's not a boy you want to cast out as punishment – he's the sort who

130

might never come back. Maybe in body, but never in spirit. Rash, she was being, and sadistic."

"For his own good though," said Cecily. "Mother knows what's best."

Perhaps fearing she may have gone too far, the housekeeper said, "Oh, certainly. Mrs Lockwood was right to say it. She's a wise woman, trying to protect her son. But the look on his face – it was tragedy. He only wants to be useful."

"Useful?" Cook sneered. "Seems to me the nitwit wants to get himself shot to bits."

"No, no," insisted the housekeeper, "he only wants to help. Now girls, look at you – muddy from noggin to tush! It's bathtime for you."

"But what happened?" May asked quickly. "What did Mr Lockwood say?"

"Well, bless, Mr Lockwood was the hero of the moment. Who knows what would have happened if Mr Lockwood hadn't been there? He went for the door, but he looked back just a second – looked at the lad, and said something quite touching. *I wish I had half your courage*, he said. And then he was gone, and if he never sees this house again I'm sorry his last memories will be such disagreeable ones –" Mrs Winter caught her tongue before it ran off once more, "– but of course he'll be home in a day or two, by which time all will be forgotten. Now you two, before that dog mistakes you for something rank to roll in: the bath!"

THE WORST OCCURS

Peregrine was gone for four days, longer than anyone had expected but not, contrary to Mrs Winter's prediction, long enough for the unpleasantness between mother and son to be forgotten. These were very still, muffled days at Heron Hall. Cecily and May spent the time wandering the house and its grounds, Byron padding amiably behind them. The house offered endless entertainments for two girls, including the provision of a flat-bottomed skiff which they dragged from the boathouse and set sail upon the lake. The herons watched their clumsy attempts to paddle from one shore to another, taking to the air when Byron, deeming the whole adventure too fraught, waded in to rescue his charges.

Mrs Lockwood would have protested as forcibly as the dog to this boating expedition, had she been able to see it;

but Heloise kept to herself during these days, holed up in her bedroom from which emerged a stream of letters addressed to her many friends. She came downstairs as usual for lunch and dinner, and was coolly polite and coolly smiling, very much her usual self: but she and Jeremy were wary of one another now, having glimpsed something of which the other was capable. Wounded and angry but also missing each other, mother and son were remindful of cats who must share a fence, a street, an entire world, and are surly about it – yet who long, too, to curl up in the warmth and security of one another, as cats and kittens yearn to do.

The girls saw Jeremy at meals and at other unscheduled moments in the day. Unaware that they knew of his humiliation in the hallway, the boy behaved toward them as he always had: standoffishly, a little patronisingly, but also with unexpected kindness. Concerned they were becoming lazy, he drew up a routine of exercises and put the children through daily paces. Troubled by the increasingly thin state of their education, he lectured them in spelling and arithmetic, and devised exams for them to sit. In the morning, when his newspaper reading was done, he accompanied them on rambles, showing them the kinds of places where artefacts and fossils could be found – in weather-exposed tree roots, in suspiciously shaped hollows, in crumbling hillsides. They found a stillborn lamb, which made Cecily cry. They viewed Snow Castle but only from a distance, as if each had secret reason for not wanting to go near. If the girls were indeed in the company of a boy who *could kill a man if he had to*, he gave no sign of his cold-hearted potential. In fact, when they discovered a raven snared in wire Jeremy put his coat over its head and worked its trembling body free; the gardener said later they should have wrung its black neck but Jeremy replied, "That would have been cruel."

When Peregrine returned on the fourth evening, the household already knew the dreadful news he would bring with him. For two days the radio and newspapers had been concerned with nothing else. What they had to report was terrifying, and a hush of grief had fallen over the country. London was under attack.

So long expected, so well prepared-for, so clearly visualized, the air raids were nonetheless completely other than what had been expected. The first assault, when it finally came, had taken place in broad daylight, late in the afternoon. The enemy had put into the air every warplane at its disposal: hundreds of them – almost a thousand – had blackened the sky over the city. Above streets and houses, doors had opened in the bellies of the bombers and the bombs had slipped free – tumbling, for an instant, fins first, then righting themselves so their blunt noses pointed to the ground, to the docks, the gardens, the playgrounds, the people. They fell with the weight of the inevitable, and boomed into their targets. London caught fire, and thousands rushed for shelter, and many did not find it.

Throughout the first afternoon and night the planes

flew, the bombs plummeted, the city burned, and the people died. And as no one believed a single attack would satisfy their enemy, no one was surprised when, the following night, the planes had returned; and the city had burned, and people had died.

Peregrine arrived home tired and drawn, limping heavily on his bad leg. A meal was brought for him in his study, and his guests sat around him, on the edges of their chairs, watching while he ate, making frivolous comments, aware of his weariness but needing to hear the awful words that must soon be said. The household staff came to the door and gathered there, likewise desperate to hear the testimony of this eyewitness, this link to the outside world.

Finally Jeremy could hedge round the subject no more: he asked, "Is it as bad as the newspapers are saying, Uncle?"

"It's as bad as you imagine." Peregrine wiped his hands and set aside the plate. "It will get worse, of course. Now it's begun – now they've decided they'll take the city in pieces, if that's the only way they can get their hands on it – they won't stop. While we lack planes built for night fighting, they won't stop. We expect they'll return tonight, and tomorrow night, and the next night, and every night. They will keep bombing us either as long as they need to, or as long as they're able."

"They will stop." Jeremy was stony. "We'll fight them out of the air. Somehow we'll do it. We'll make them sorry."

Cecily spoke from where she had hidden behind Byron. "What was it like, Uncle Peregrine?"

"Frightening," the man said simply. "It stops your heart to watch a squadron cut across the sky, so tidy, so efficient, so dutiful, a sight which would make you proud if you didn't know that inside those planes are men whose task it is to pound you into bits. It stops your breath to know that no place is more secure than another – a cathedral no safer than a tenement – and that it's only dumb luck if you're standing where the bomb doesn't land, or standing where it does. Your existence is stripped down to nothing but chance. Everything you've ever hoped, believed, achieved – all of it is less meaningful than dust, it can't help you, it won't spare you, if your feet have you standing in precisely the wrong place."

His audience watched in silence as the speaker reached for his glass and took a drink.

"The noise freezes your blood," he continued. "The fighter planes make a thrumming noise, like very furious bees; the bombers make a heavier roar which sounds louder in your head than in actuality, a noise that cavemen might have recognized. That first afternoon, the shadows of the planes flicked along the ground fast, like racing demons, crossing roads and leaping walls. When each shadow passed, you could breathe for a moment, then wait for the next one to come. Finally the sun went out and the shadows disappeared, and it was a mercy, really. To be rid of those spectral messengers."

Heloise's sights drifted without mooring. "God help us," she whispered.

Peregrine took a cigarette out of its case and held it to the flame Jeremy hastened to light. "Bombs make, so I'm told, a soft howl as they fall, but I never heard that. I only heard what comes after the howl: the boom as a building explodes. And shouting and screaming in the streets. The honking of horns, the thud of running feet. And the wail of sirens – air-raid sirens, ambulance sirens, fire-engine sirens, police sirens – yowling on and on without cease, telling everyone what we already knew."

"And the damage? What did you see?"

Peregrine paused, smoke curling from his fingers. "It's funny, you know – I've never seen a bomb site, yet what I saw tallied exactly with what I pictured in my head – exactly, no doubt, as you picture in yours. What's a building when it's destroyed? They are made of brick and timber, as we are muscle and bone. Plain things, but alive and working together, as they're designed to, they have elegance, they have – soul. And maybe there's nothing so lifeless, so finished, as something that has had its soul torn away. The rubble is ugly. It's made of chunks of brick, a trillion chips of glass, smashed and splintered timber. All this sprawls over the roads, into the gutters, heaps against its neighbours. Caught in the mess is furniture, carpet, birdcages, pots and pans, chests of drawers filled with clothes. Stinking dust floats everywhere, and the dirt ripped up by the impact is thrown over everything. And where the building once stood there's an odd empty space, and light touches what it never touched before, and sparrows hop along towel rails, and dogs walk on roofs."

"Oh," breathed Cecily.

Peregrine ashed and smoked his cigarette. "We can expect them to bomb hospitals, libraries, churches, museums, important places like that. They'll try to break our spirit by taking away what we need and care about."

"Oh," said Cecily again. She imagined the stuffed animals from the museum blowing sky-high, zebras and gnus and sloths and anteaters soaring to the clouds amid a glittering shower of glass.

"And the people?" It was Mrs Winter, the housekeeper. "I don't mind about the buildings – what about the people?"

Peregrine said, "Hundreds died, that first afternoon and night – maybe five hundred or more. A countless number were injured. The next night, fewer were lost; we were better prepared. But while the raids continue, many people will die. There's no doubting that."

"But what about the shelters? What about the windows being blacked out?"

"The shelters will save people. The blackout will save people. Every small defence will help."

Cecily remembered the window in her London bedroom, its crisscross of tape and shrouding of curtain. She remembered her father standing at the window and looking through a gap in the drapes. With a sense of helpless falling she realized how flimsy a defence against a bomb was the curtain of a girl's bedroom. "Is my Daddy safe?" she asked.

"Humphrey is safe. Your house is safe. And May. . ." Peregrine looked to the child who crouched by the couch saying nothing, fiercely focused on every word, "your home is safe too."

"Today," mused Mrs Winter. "We are safe for today."

The many occupants of the room and doorway gazed dully into space, as if the conversation had delivered to each of them a stunning blow to the head. Heloise was the first to speak. "So," she sighed, "what now? What dreadful thing must happen next?"

Peregrine smoked his cigarette and smoke drifted around him, between his elegant fingers and through his mane of hair. He shrugged and smiled. "We'll fight, as Jeremy says. Now this battle has begun, we can start winning it. People will get up in the morning, go to work as usual, feed their families, walk in the park. No one will panic or lose hope. They will only beat us when we let them."

"Yes." Mrs Winter approved. "Business as usual. Carry on." And began doing so immediately, shuffling the staff away from the door and back to their evening tasks.

Left alone in the study, the family found there wasn't anything to say. The subject of the air raids could have continued all night, but there was nothing that, added now, could vitally improve on what had been said. Heloise, who

139

liked silence, nevertheless felt compelled to break this one: "You must be tired, Peregrine."

"A little," her brother-in-law admitted.

"I'm angry," said Jeremy. "I'm so angry." His fists were closed, his lovely eyes hard, but he was ignored. Everyone was angry; no one assumed he was angrier than most.

Cecily raised her head above the parapet of Byron's ears. "Will you tell us more about the Duke, Uncle?"

"Oh no," tisked her mother, "no disagreeable stories tonight. . ."

Peregrine seemed about to agree with her; then said, "Why not? History repeats itself: the battle for power is fought over and over again. We *should* hear from our Duke tonight. We might learn something from him."

FROM DUKE TO VILLAIN

"Where were we?" asked the storyteller, who knew perfectly well. "Our Duke has watched his family battle its way to the throne. His brother is king and the father of many children, including two fine princes. The Duke's second brother, Clarence, has been put to death. Both the King and the royal children are thoroughly under the Queen's control. The Duke and the Queen venomously hate each other, but the King stands between them, his very existence keeping the pair from flying at each other's throats.

"And then something happens to change the game."

"The King dies!" crowed Cecily.

"The King died. And why not? A king is flesh and blood. A crown, a sceptre, a uniform, an army, boundless ambition, overweening pride: these things don't make a man a god. The

King died as a man must die: long live the King! And who, now, was the King? Little Edward, the first-born son, twelve short years old.

"We haven't spoken much of this boy, but he is crucial to this story – indeed, though we've said so much about our Duke, it's the boy who stands at the heart of this tale, a diamond under so much coal. Prince Edward has grown up far from court – far from his mother and father, who seem to have loved him although they kept him in a castle in the kingdom's distant south. Here he had been raised by the Queen's family, who gave him an excellent education and appear to have produced a gracious child. All reports describe the Prince as polite and gentle, perhaps a touch grave. He was clever, a reader of books; pious, a child of faith; as well as a sportsman – he could swing a sword, hunt with hounds, play skilful games. Some say he was sickly, with disease turning in his bones: if so, it didn't prevent him from living up to the demands of being both prince and boy. He resembled his pretty mother, and not just in beauty: surrounded by the Queen's family, it was her influence he lived under, her thoughts which became his, her distrusts, suspicions and allegiances which he took up as his own. The Queen was crafting the Prince into a future king who would favour her line above all others, staking her family's claim not just on her son's crown, but on the crowns of kings to come.

"It could only have made the Duke uneasy. This boy, his own nephew, this future king, secreted away in the south and being reared by those the Duke despised, and who despised him in return. This puppet who would come to power as sure as night follows day.

"And now, unexpectedly, the King was dead. Like a hawk swooping out of nowhere, the critical moment arrived. The chain which had always kept the enemies at bay snapped with a twang: now one faction must pull the heart from its rival and obliterate it utterly, or have the same done to them. The Queen had already had a hand in getting rid of one of the King's brothers. There was no reason she wouldn't try to do the same to the brother who remained. But our Duke was no reckless fool, as Clarence had been. He was cunning, a wolf. And the King, before he died, had done a remarkable thing. Wanting, perhaps, to hobble the ambition of the Queen's family, on his deathbed he had written a new will. In it he named the Duke protector of the nation and guardian of the royal children until the time when the young King Edward came of age."

Jeremy smiled. "Power."

"Power! Our insatiable friend rears its Medusa head. As you can imagine, the Queen was not amused to hear this news. She had no intention of handing her offspring, let alone the nation, into the care of her enemy. Twisting and turning to get a grip on her rival's throat, she discovered that, according to law, the Duke could only stand as protector until the day the new king was crowned. Thus were plans drawn up instantly for the coronation. The Prince was

143

summoned from his castle in all haste, under the escort of two thousand men.

"But our Duke, in his own far-flung castle, was not without friends at court, most of whom feared for their futures if the Queen's cronies seized power. They wrote to the Duke, urging him into action which they promised to support. *Strike now*, they advised, *while the iron is hot*.

"And the Duke did not tarry: he struck. Some say he acted in desperation, out of genuine fear for his life; others say that everything he does from now on is a calculated step on a ruthless climb to the top. I shall leave you to decide for yourselves which is more likely true.

"Quickly, while the two thousand men were amassing around the Prince, the Duke gathered his supporters, men of strength and standing. He wrote nice letters pledging his loyalty to the new king. When he finally set out, it was in the company of a black-clad army and one precarious, astonishing plan.

"So now we have the Duke travelling downwind and the Prince travelling upwind, both riding towards a collision only one of them knows will happen. The Duke sends a message to the Prince's guardians, suggesting the parties rendezvous along the road. The Queen sends a message to these same guardians, urging them to speed the Prince to London without delay. But the Duke is not a man whom mere guardians may snub; besides, he has written those nice letters. So the leaders of each party meet to dine in a village, but not before the Prince is lodged, by the nervous guardians, at an inn some miles away. This act of rudeness – the hiding of the nephew from the uncle – was greeted by the Duke with perfect understanding and calm.

"The meal lasted long into the night, and was very merry – long and merry enough for the Prince's guardians to be addle-headed on retirement to their beds. Whereupon the Duke locked their doors from the outside, and, as dawn arrived, galloped with his army to meet the boy at his inn. The child was glad to see his uncle, if a little baffled as to the whereabouts of his guardians. The Duke confessed that, most unfortunately, he had had to arrest them. They weren't men to be trusted, the Duke explained. The Prince believed otherwise, and protested; the Duke tut-tutted but added that he would now, also unfortunately, arrest those men who remained by the Prince's side. The servants and officers, the teachers and close friends, all the people who'd surrounded and cared for the Prince his whole life, were to disappear immediately and forever, under pain of death.

"Finding himself captured and isolated, young Edward discovered that being a prince, and even a king, doesn't change the fact that you are, in your skin, just a boy. He did, now, what any boy might do: he put his hands to his face and cried."

Peregrine settled back in his chair, seeming as relieved as the Duke might have been to have reached this point in the story. Trays of cocoa had been brought, and he stirred his with a teaspoon. Cecily, snuggled up to the dog, watched him closely. Without meaning to, she had started to picture her uncle as the Duke. Her Uncle Peregrine, partaking of a merry meal. Her Uncle Peregrine, glaring down at a boy king. Uncle Peregrine, crafting a plan out of pieces like glowing arrows of glass.

"It's a kind of terrible chess, isn't it?" said Jeremy. "The Duke has toppled the white pawns, the white rooks, the white bishops and the white knights. He's cornered the white king. The queen is still on the board, but she's in a bad position now. Check."

"That's clever, Jem," said his mother; but her son did not return her smile.

"*Check* is one word," Peregrine agreed. "*Bloodless coup* are two more. Now that the Duke had the Prince in his clutches, power shifted titanically away from the Queen and into the arms of the Duke. The Queen remembered a thousand reasons she'd given the Duke to think badly of her. Fearful, outraged, she looked for support, and discovered that people weren't willing to give it: she and her gang had fewer true friends than they realized. So the Queen did the only thing she could do now: she gathered her children – yes, including Princess Cecily – and went into sanctuary in the Abbey."

"What is sanctuary?"

"Sanctuary is a place which no one may enter with violent intent. Nobody may harm or seize a person who is in sanctuary, even if that person is a criminal. While someone is in sanctuary, they are absolutely safe; but they are also trapped. Sanctuary's protection does not extend beyond the sanctified walls, so the sanctuary-seeker dare not leave. . . By the next morning, the Duke's men had surrounded the Abbey. The Queen might hide; but her hidey-hole would be her prison.

"If the people disliked the Queen, it's true they weren't too keen on the Duke, either. As news of the coup spread, anxious crowds began to gather in the streets. The lords and councillors were also worried, as many had reason to be: they'd simpered and cooed around the Queen for years. But the Duke, still miles away on the road, wrote letters assuring everyone that he'd captured the Prince only to ensure his own safety, that he had no violent intent, that neither the country nor the boy had anything to fear. Seeing how the land lay – the Queen's party so weakened, the Duke's star on the rise – many people stopped cheering for the Queen, and started cheering for the Duke. That happens, of course. Acts of tyranny – which is what the Duke's actions should properly be called – are often deemed understandable, even forgivable, by those who might benefit from them.

"So the Duke rode in triumph into the city, weeping the loss of the old king, trumpeting the advent of the new. The Queen's family had been torn from power like strangling ivy from a tree: everything, now, could be good again. A pressing need was to find somewhere to house the Prince, and the place chosen was the Tower."

"The Tower of London?" said May. "I've been there."

Cecily vaguely remembered something she'd been taught at school. "That Tower is a horrible place, isn't it, Uncle?"

"The Tower was old even back then," Peregrine replied, "but it wasn't decayed or ramshackle, and it didn't cast a fearful shadow, as it would do in later centuries. Rather, it was a royal residence, with views across the river, manicured gardens and a zoo, and lavish rooms where the Prince's father, like kings before him, had hosted important meetings and banquets. In short, it was a suitably luxurious, familiar, and safe place for the boy. He was given a suite of chambers with stained-glass windows and prancing animals painted on the walls; he was given some servants and attendants; and of course he was given some guards.

"The date set for the Prince's coronation was coming near – too near for the Duke's liking, so he put it back another month, and used the extra time to make himself grand, lathering himself with titles, gorging himself on importance. The one cloud on his horizon was the Queen and her offspring sulking in sanctuary. It looked bad—"

"It makes the Duke look scary!" Cecily's understanding amazed even herself.

"Exactly," said Peregrine. "The Queen's hiding makes the Duke seem a man best kept away from. So he tries to coax the family out, and the Queen refuses, which is embarrassing and inconvenient. Time's ticking, as it always is for the Duke. Soon his reign as protector will end: the Prince will be brought from the Tower in a fury, the Queen will come snarling out of sanctuary, the boy will finally be crowned; and no one will be the Duke's friend then, no one will want to side with one who has so offended the King. But that day hasn't arrived, and for now the Duke has the support of the people and of well-placed men. He has ships and countless soldiers at his command, he has imprisoned his enemies, and he has, most of all, the boy in the Tower.

"And the choice the Duke faces is this: hand all of this over on the day of the coronation, and wait for the retaliation that will certainly come . . . or don't. Don't give anything back. Throw caution to the wind, grab the chance while it is there, regret nothing, keep everything, and try to get more."

"Keep everything," Cecily advised.

Peregrine smiled bleakly. "The Duke makes his choice. Once made, there's no retreat. The road forward is remorseless and bloody: but the Duke was born by this roadside, he has walked it all his life. Treachery, conspiracy, victory-or-death, *might is right*: he learned it in his cradle. As a child, he saw his brother snatch the crown from the old sick king. And now the time has come for the Duke to snatch the crown from a child.

"It is not a decision which calls for a delicate touch. He summons his army from the north, soldiers he can trust. He chops heads from those who might object to his decision, including some owned by men who'd once been his friends. He does not bother with truths, trials, or any such niceties, and why should he? He isn't playing games. A dark fire is burning in him, the flame which, once lit, must consume everything, including the heart that kindled it.

"For the Prince in the Tower, the Duke's decision came like a stormcloud. His attendants were sent away, so only the guards remained. He heard about – perhaps, from his windows, he even witnessed – the lopping of heads. A quiet boy, a contemplative boy, he understood the meaning of these events. And he became quieter, and downcast. He was very clever, that boy – clever enough to be afraid."

"I feel sorry for him," said Cecily. The Prince was twelve, she herself was twelve: it made her feel she knew him better than did anyone else in the room.

"Children have always borne the brunt of decisions made by adults," said Peregrine. "No child is responsible for the bombs that will fall on London tonight, but plenty will pay a dreadful price nonetheless."

Jeremy said, "Children have no power, that's why."

"Children are almost always powerless, you're correct. And children aren't something that powerful people often take into consideration. But *this* child was the King's son. This child was *to be* king. The Duke had him isolated and imprisoned, helpless; yet the child shadowed every moment of the man's life. And not just this child, either. There was another of whom we've hardly spoken, but who likewise preyed on the Duke's mind. The Prince had a brother, remember? A brother younger by several years, second in line

150

to the throne. His name was Richard. The Prince was like a fly bundled up in the Duke's web: but as long as Richard existed, likely at any moment to step forward and claim his birthright, the Duke's stake on the crown would never be secure.

"This little boy Richard, nine years old, was living with his mother in sanctuary, where the Duke's claws couldn't reach. The Duke had tried to wheedle out the child, saying the lad must attend the coronation, saying the Prince needed a playmate, saying the child should not be a prisoner of sanctuary. His mother had refused to let the boy go. The Duke was her enemy, and thus the enemy of her children. So the Duke did what had always worked for him before. He sent the Queen a message *insisting* that she send the child out for the coronation. Looking beyond the window, the Queen saw hundreds of soldiers encircling the Abbey, a hint of what the Duke's response to yet another refusal would be."

"Might is right," said Jeremy.

"What a lesson to be teaching, Peregrine. . ."

Jeremy looked at his mother with scorn. "Uncle Peregrine isn't teaching it. We already know it. We only have to open a newspaper to see the proof of it. Isn't Germany doing exactly what the Duke did, hammering away at us with threats and bombs – and the Queen doing exactly as we are, hunkering down, refusing to be afraid?"

"Well, I think your father could explain the difference—"

"It's the same thing." Jeremy turned away dismissively.

Peregrine shook a cigarette from the pack and lit it, making no comment on the rift between mother and son. He said, "The Queen, seeing those soldiers, saw she had no choice. The child was handed over, and some say he wept and hated to leave his mama, and some say he was overjoyed to escape the confines of the Abbey and be united with his brother."

"Probably a bit of both," said Cecily.

A small voice spoke up: it belonged to May Bright. "Did they know each other, those brothers? The Prince had always lived in his castle in the south. His brother had always lived with his mother in the palace. Weren't they strangers?"

"An interesting point," admitted Peregrine. "I suppose that, even if they didn't know each other well, they knew they could be friends."

"Like you and me, May! We were strangers, now we're friends. Children like being with other children."

"I wonder," mused Jeremy. "I wonder if the Prince was really happy to see him."

"Of course he was! Why wouldn't he have been? *I* would have been happy to see *you*, Jem—"

"But *I* wouldn't have been happy to see *you*, Cecily – don't you get it? The Prince was smart. He knew he was in a dangerous place. Now his brother was in that place too."

Cecily rolled her eyes. "I *do* get it," she said. "But even though the Prince was smart, he was still a boy. He would have been glad to see someone his own age. Someone to talk to. Someone to play with. Wouldn't you have been *sort-of* glad to see me?"

"No," said Jeremy.

Cecily stuck out her tongue and turned her back to him. "Keep telling the story, Uncle Peregrine."

Peregrine's gaze had fallen; the last few days had been harrowing, and he was exhausted. "They did play," he said. "Some people claim to have seen the brothers playing together in the gardens in the days after Richard joined his brother. By now the Duke was also living in the Tower. He'd taken the Prince's grand chamber as his own, and moved the boys deeper into the building, into the Keep. The rooms of the Keep were very fine, but they were also impossible to escape. They had been used to hold important prisoners in the past; now, they did so again. The walls of the Keep were thicker than a man is tall; and no one could see into the windows, and no one could see out. Soon sightings of the princes in the gardens grew sparse, and petered out; and soon the two children were never seen outside, in the sunshine, again."

A FIT OF GLOOM

Newspapers: always newspapers, with their dirty inky smell and their vague dustiness, taking up too much of the breakfast table and catching her uncle's eye as if he were a sailor and they that singing mermaid on the rock. Jeremy was different: he could lose himself in the pages all day for all Cecily cared, although anyone could see that reading about bombs and aeroplanes wasn't doing him any good. Her uncle, however, was another matter. Cecily felt physical pain to have Peregrine so near, and yet to be ignored. She glared across the table, psychically willing him to lower the paper and talk. The newspaper shielded him like a jealous girl obscuring the stare of a rival. "Uncle Peregrine!" she finally squawked.

"Mmm?"

Immediately Cecily realized she had nothing specific to say. "What's. . . What's happening?" she asked, though she could see for herself. LONDON HIT HARD OVERNIGHT read the headlines. It chilled her to know they were talking about her own city, where her home was, where her father was.

"What's happening is an outrage," muttered Peregrine, and shook straight the sagging paper.

Cecily glanced at May, who sat with her back to the windows. The morning sun came through the glass and spangled around the edges of the evacuee. The sky behind her was a watercolour blue. "It's going to be a nice day," Cecily observed.

"We can play outside," said May.

"After lessons." Cecily looked at her brother. "What will we learn today, Jem?"

He frowned, proving he'd heard something, but his attention stayed on the newspaper. "I'm not sure. Maybe later."

May smiled; Cecily felt glum. She heaped raspberry jam on a slice of toast, so much that it plastered her nose with redness as it passed underneath. It took time to consume this monster, during which Jeremy made several comments on the air raids but failed to notice his sister's indelicacy. "Uncle," said Cecily, when she'd unstuck her teeth and could speak again, "those two princes in the Tower. Why have they disappeared?"

It was something which had troubled her as she'd readied herself for bed the previous night, that Peregrine had ended the second instalment of the Duke's story at the point of the brothers' vanishing from view. It was not a settled place to park the telling, and had left her feeling frustrated. "What's happened to them? Are they dead?"

A victory: Peregrine actually glanced past the newspaper. "The story is more than four hundred and fifty years old. Everyone in it is dead."

"You know what I mean! Tell us what's happened."

"Not now."

"Aww! Please? You might have to go away again, and not come back for days. . ."

"Well, a story that's waited nearly five centuries can easily wait a few days."

Cecily slumped. Jeremy turned a page, and Cecily's disappointed eye fell on a photograph in a corner of the newspaper. A woman and a child stood beside a mountain of hideous rubble. From the way they were standing, the way they were staring, one could tell the rubble had been their house. Craning closer, she read the caption. *Alex, aged 7, sobs and says, "I can't find my cat!"*

"Oh!" Cecily's eyes went swimmy. "Don't worry little boy, you'll find your cat! He's got nine lives, remember?"

After breakfast the girls did the skipping, hopping and press-ups which would keep their minds healthy and their bodies ready for action. Then they tumbled out into the day, which was not as warm as it looked, and made their daily rounds of the outbuildings. May said they might find a tramp asleep in the barn; Cecily wasn't sure she wanted to. She was ready to run as May poked about in the hay with a pitchfork. A moth flew up, but no pronged tramp screamed. Finally, "You might as well stop," Cecily said. "There's nobody here."

"Hmm," said May.

Cecily changed the subject. "I'm worried about Daddy. Those horrible bombs. Are you worried about your mum?"

May didn't dignify the question with an answer, only hung the fork on the wall. A pigeon had come to the door of the barn and was sunning itself in a square of light. May waggled her fingers at it, and it looked back with a scarlet stare. Idly she said, "If your daddy is so important, he'll be safe. They won't let bombs fall on important people's heads."

"Won't they?"

"No. It's like what my mum says about France: all the fancy generals stay far away, only the ordinary soldiers get shot. Only ordinary people will get squished by bombs. All the important people will be safe."

Cecily thought on this, reasoned it was probably true. It was necessary to keep the important people safe, because otherwise important things would no longer get done. The pigeon had waddled off, flecks of hay were floating through the sunshine. "What shall we do now?" she asked.

"Let's play sanctuary," said May.

"Yeah! How do we play that?"

"We'll go to Snow Castle, and that can be sanctuary, and I'll be the Duke and you can be the Queen, and you can hide, and I'll try to make you come out."

"OK!" Cecily went for the door – then caught herself, turning back with a bashful face. "Do we have to play in Snow Castle? Can't we play here? I'm a bit scared of Snow Castle," she admitted.

May the fearless replied, "It's only an old ruin. It just makes funny echoes. It can't hurt you."

"What about those boys?"

"Those boys weren't there last time. They've probably gone home. It's been days and days."

"Uh," said Cecily, convinced, yet unconvinced. "Shall we bring Byron?"

"Yes! Then when I'm the Duke, he can be my army."

So they located and chivvied the Newfoundland from his place at his master's feet, changed their shoes for wellingtons and ran out into the field, May speeding about like a fighter plane, Cecily lumbering like a bomber. "Get away from me, get away from me!" she shrilled at the evacuee, getting into character as the Queen; in reply May laughed connivingly, and tossed her glossy head. In the woods she found a good stick which would serve as a sword; naturally Cecily also required a prop, so May yanked a length of weed from around an elm's trunk and fashioned it into a crown.

They romped into the morning, two girls who easily forgot that the world was tearing apart at the seams. They slogged across the far field with the usual sense of being the last people alive, crossed the river with the typical dunking of feet, climbed the bank with the required muddying of knees. Snow Castle stood, devastated as ever, beautiful in the cream light. Sunlight shafted between gaps in the stone, twinkled on chips of white marble. May and Cecily stopped and stared. "It's lovely, isn't it?" Cecily couldn't fathom how something so festery and broken could be so spectacular.

"It's strange. Most of the castle has gone, but – it *feels* like it's here, doesn't it?"

Cecily believed she knew what May meant. Although most of Snow Castle's walls and all of its roof were missing, their very absence told of things that had been. It was impossible to look at the ruin and not envisage the turrets, the countless rooms, the sweeping stairways, the massive arched doors. And all these seemed *here* rather more than they *weren't here*. . . It was odd. It was as if the destructions and disappearances of time had caused the castle no real inconvenience at all.

With a wave of her hand May gestured that the Queen should seek the safety of sanctuary. "Go in where I can't reach you."

Cecily took four or five steps forward, and stalled. Even this short distance into the depths of the ruin made her feel enveloped by stone, and alone. She looked back. "Is this far enough?"

"That's good, just stand there. Now you are the Queen in sanctuary. Come out, you hag!"

May yelled these last words, startling Cecily. Then, grinning, the Queen howled back, "Never, you beast! I don't trust you as far as I can spit! A pox on you, wicked Duke!"

May danced about. "A pox?"

"That's what I said, a pox!"

"What's a pox?"

"I don't know! It's a kind of cage—"

"That's a box!"

"Oh, I don't care, a pox *and* a box!"

"Listen to me, Queeny!" May shook her sword. "You have to come out. You're embarrassing me. You're making me look bad."

"You are bad! It serves you right if you're embarrassed. I'm never coming out. I like it here in sanctuary. It's very snug."

"I can make it *not* snug. . ."

"No you can't, you can't touch me, not while I'm in sanctuary!" The Queen actually thumbed her nose, an act unbecoming of royalty. "You're a sneaky man, and you've kidnapped my son. If my husband the King were here, he'd wring your neck!"

"But the King's not here!" shouted the Duke, who felt the Queen was running off with the show. "He's as dead as a dodo—"

"Ha ha!" The Queen pounced. "The dodo isn't dead yet, dummy!"

The girls stared at each other, stunned by this uncharacteristic brilliance on Cecily's part. "Well, the King isn't here," said May lamely, "and now I'm going to – to – send in the bear!" She waved the sword at Byron. "Fetch her, loyal bear! Grab the hag by the hair!"

But Byron was sniffing an arena of grass where fox cubs had tussled during the night, and did not answer the call of duty beyond a noncommittal wave of his tail. "Go!" said May, slashing her sword; the magnificent tail waved. "Oh bear!" cried May, feeling her material growing thin. "What can you smell? Is it the blood of my poor brother Clarence?"

"I hope so," cackled the Queen. "I'm glad he's dead dead dead!"

"I'm not," said May, and there was something in her voice that Cecily might have noticed, a quaver, a pulled thread, as if she had sympathy for all those who pay a heavy price for rash decisions – had not Byron, at that instant, flung up his head and barked. His hair went electric, his white fangs showed, he transformed into a creature more ferocious than any bear. Cecily and May sprang away, but even as they leapt it was clear the dog wasn't barking at them. His blazing eyes were fixed on something which hovered somewhere behind Cecily, in the core of the ruin.

It was May who gathered her wits first, and hastened to scoop her arms around the dog's neck. "Shh, By-By! It's only that boy!"

It was the younger one, watching them resentfully as if they were the intruders, not he. Cecily glared, hardly believing her eyes. "You!" she said.

161

"Me," the child replied.

May hugged Byron. "You gave us a fright!"

"That dog did," the child corrected. "I don't care for that dog."

"The dog doesn't care for you," said Cecily. There was an arrogance about this boy that brought out a remorselessness in her, and she felt no guilt in allowing it free rein, but rather a primitive satisfaction. Some instinct, much older than her twelve years, warned her that she must not let the boy, these boys, lull her. "Where's your brother?" she asked.

"Would you rather talk to him?"

"Not particularly. I'm just wondering where he is."

The child smiled, leaned his head against a wall. He was wearing his florid outfit of velvet and linen, and his long fawn hair hung in groomed ringlets. "People always want to talk to my brother. Never to me."

"I'm not surprised."

"Sometimes *I'd* like to be the special one."

Cecily, second-born and, she frequently suspected, second-best, was taken aback. "I know how you feel," she had to admit.

"*Do* you?" He looked up. "Why do you?"

"I've got an older brother too. You're not the only one."

The child thought this over. "Does he talk of things you don't care about? Does he sometimes say, *Go away, I must think?*"

"All the time," said Cecily.

"We are friends then!" chirruped the child: and the smile he gave Cecily was so endearing, so vibrant and full of willingness and invitation to play, that the wary instinct inside her seemed misguided, like the good dog in the tale of the hobgoblins. Indeed, in the boy's smile Cecily remembered things she had forgotten: toys long lost, cuddles from her mother, the taste of biscuits she'd chewed as a baby. It was very odd, yet it made her want to be his friend.

The good dog who stood beside her, however, was not so easily won over. Byron continued to growl at the boy. The child hardly glanced at the animal, but May saw that he kept the dog in the corner of his eye. "Where is your brother?" she asked. "Are you alone?"

He smiled again – secretive and knowing, this time – and looked over his shoulder. "They can't see you," he said, and his brother was suddenly there, beside his sibling; and both girls had the confusing sense that he'd always been there, in the shadows, but that somehow they'd been unable to notice him.

Like the child, the older boy was wearing an elegant outfit of navy velvet. His long hair shone cleanly, and his face, porcelain-pale, was blushed with pink life. Together, the brothers made Cecily think of pretty dolls which never had left a glass cabinet; which were, perhaps, locked in the cabinet, in a locked attic, high up in the roof space of a boarded-up and forgotten house. The older boy stared dubiously at the Newfoundland: "Brother," he muttered, "come away."

"Sit down, Byron! That's enough!" With the big dog quietened, Cecily said to the pair, "Why are you still here? Weren't you escaping from your hosts and running back to your mother?"

"We still wish to go home. But it's only a dream."

Cecily snorted. "You could at least *try*. You haven't tried very hard, have you? All this time and you haven't taken one *step* closer to home."

The boy dropped his gaze. "I should do better," he admitted. "But we are watched, as I told you. The roads are watched. If we are caught, we will be punished."

"Who will punish you? Your host family? We've heard that some people are treating their evacuees poorly, making them work on the farm and clean floors – is that what your hosts have been doing? Have they whipped you? Are they starving you? Have they beat you with a stick?"

"Silence!" The younger child jabbed a sudden finger at Cecily. "You said your father would save us!"

"I meant he will save us *in the war*, you goose. He can't save you from scrubbing the floors, he's too. . ." Cecily stopped short of using the word *important*. She should have been proud, yet she hesitated. "He's busy with big things, like battles. Not small things, like children."

The taller boy's curls tumbled as he shook his head. "It no longer matters," he said. "It's too late for us now. I had hopes, but I have given up hoping. Everything is lost."

"No, no, all is not lost!" The child clutched his brother's

shoulder as if to prevent him from sliding irretrievably away. "All isn't lost! You still have me!"

"Yes, I have you." The boy smiled faintly at Cecily and May. "Sometimes I wish I didn't. If it were just myself here, I would not fear. They could do with me as they please—"

"Don't say this! Oh, don't lose heart!"

"– but I must protect my brother. That is my single duty now. And it is dangerous to leave this place. Dangerous to go home; yet dangerous to stay."

Cecily pawed the grass. Inside her boiled a perplexing brew of feelings for these two. They infuriated and fascinated her, made her feel strong but also ignorant. "Home is dangerous because of the bombs? Of course it's dangerous! But my daddy is in London, and May's mum is there, and thousands of other people are there—"

"We don't trust strangers," said the child.

"Arh!" Cecily kicked out; the weedy crown, riding forgotten on her head, flopped into the grass. "I'm not talking about *strangers*! I'm saying, other people are being brave! You should stop making excuses and just admit that you are scared! Scaredy-cats, is what you are – you're nothing but two little chickens!"

From their corner the brothers stared at her in astonishment. The crown caught Cecily's eye, and she stomped on it. It snagged on her wellington, clung to her foot; another good stomp crushed it utterly. May said something, and Cecily swung to her. "What? What?"

165

"They're only children," said the girl.

Stoked by frustration, Cecily puffed like a train. Byron was on his feet; she gripped his ear to calm herself. "I know that," she grumbled. "But it's still true."

The older boy spoke. He was holding his brother's hand. "It is true," he admitted, and his voice was like the skeleton of a leaf, his smile a cradle for all the sorrow history has known. "I am afraid. I was brought up to be bold, to know my mind, to believe I wouldn't fail: but all I am is what you say. I'm nothing but a frightened boy."

GAMES TO PLAY

Now that this truth had been admitted, Cecily should have felt better. She had scored a victory – both boys actually seemed slighter, smaller, faded – yet victory was hollow. These two were merely fancy-dressed waifs, two homeless white mice: berating them was as nasty as striking a pup. "It's all right to be frightened," she sighed. "I'm frightened too, sometimes."

The children didn't speak for some moments, as children don't when their hearts are beating hard and they must soothe their own feelings if they are to stay friends. Finally May said, "Some days we've come to Snow Castle, but you haven't been here. Where do you go, when you're not here?"

"We go where we can't be seen," answered the child.

Cecily would endure no more cryptic guff. "And when you're there, what do you do?"

"We talk. We pray."

"Ah," said Cecily.

". . . You don't care for talking?"

"You love talking," said May.

"It depends what I'm talking about," said Cecily.

"Do you pray?"

"Mmm, when I want something."

May announced, "I believe in Heaven."

The boy's glance flew to her. "The place of the fathers," he said.

Cecily moved on. "What else do you do?"

"We tell each other stories. We walk as far as is safe. We watch the birds, the rooks, the swallows. Birds lead interesting lives."

Cecily refrained from rolling her eyes. "And what about when you're hungry? How do you get food?"

"I used to eat and *eat*," blurted the younger enthusiastically.

"Our needs are fewer now," his brother said.

Cecily grimaced. "Don't you ever do what other boys do? Don't you run and jump? Don't you – wrestle? Don't you – throw things around?"

The small boy looked at his sibling, and for the first time his face was lit as a child's should be, with all the brightness of excitement. "Can I tell them? Let me tell them."

"If you wish," his brother said.

"We have great battles!" The little one shouted it. "We

168

each have ships, big warships with sails, and sometimes we are enemies and sometimes we are friends, and we have battles and the battles can rage for days! And sometimes I jump on his ship and stab him, and sometimes he knocks my ship to pieces, and it's my favourite game! I have a hat!"

He reached to his head to brandish this hat, dropped his hand on discovering it wasn't there. His grin, however, did not falter: "Warships is my favourite game."

"We also play army," prompted his brother.

"Yes, with swords and horses! If I capture his flag, I win! Army is good, but warships is better. When I grow up, I shall be a sailor."

"And do you wrestle? Do you fight and yell, like other boys do?"

"All the time!" shrieked the child joyously. "I scratch and kick! Would you like to play?"

"No thanks," said Cecily. "I don't play like that."

"You were playing something, though." The older boy eyed them shrewdly. "We saw you. We heard you."

"Sanctuary," said May. "It's a game we made up. Cecily was a queen hiding in sanctuary, and I was a duke trying to make her come out."

The brothers shifted in the shadows; in their dark velvet they melded into the gloom so well that, for an instant, they vanished completely. "That sounds," said the boy, "like a serious game. Not one I should very much care to play."

"It was only a game," said May. "Not real."

The child pointed a sullen finger. "She doesn't look like a queen."

"I'm dressed for rambling!" Cecily squeaked. "The wind's been blowing my hair!"

"He's teasing you," said May.

"I'm not. She doesn't."

"Hurgh!" Cecily could suddenly no longer be bothered. "I don't look like a queen because I'm *not* a queen, just like *you* don't look like a sailor because you're only a fat little pig." And, as her internal clock was striking gongs, she added, "Come on, May, let's go home. It's lunchtime."

Byron followed his mistress willingly; May paused. She might have asked any other pair of strays if they needed money or the materials to write a letter or if she should bring them some more food: but she didn't ask such things of these two. There were countless questions she would have *liked* to ask, a symphony of strange queries which, given answers, might have made her sleep more soundly . . . but Cecily was yelling, "Come *on*, May! Timeliness is the rule, remember?" and she let her questions go like leaf-boats on a river, never to be seen again. "We'll come back another day," she promised, and ran away through the grass. When she looked back, the brothers had vanished. A raven stood at the highest peak of the ruins, leaning into the wind.

For some time Cecily said nothing. The girls and the dog forded the river and climbed the bank. A slug stuck to May's palm, and they giggled and cringed about this. In the woods, where the artwork of branches gave them privacy, Cecily ventured to say, "They're very clean, those boys. For boys living outdoors, they're very clean."

"Hmm," said May.

"I don't think boys who live outside could manage to stay that clean. I think they could only be that clean if they were staying somewhere out of the weather. Maybe a barn. Maybe an empty house."

"I don't know," said May.

"They *have to* be. They can't live in the ruins. Nobody could do that."

"Hmm," repeated May.

Cecily's hand floated from tree to tree. "May?"

"What?"

"Do you think we should tell someone about those boys?"

". . . Tell who?"

"Well. We could tell my mother."

"I don't think so."

"But maybe it would help them? Mama could talk to their hosts, tell them that they're supposed to treat children kindly. . ."

May kept her eyes on Byron, who ambled ahead. The dog was pleased to leave the ruins. He did not sniff about, but made a beeline for Heron Hall, glancing back frequently to check his charges weren't dallying. "I don't think it's a good idea."

Cecily stuck out her lip, said nothing.

"Remember when the grocer told us some evacuees were running away?"

"Yes."

"Your mother didn't feel sorry for them."

"I remember." Cecily sighed.

But May wasn't finished. "She'll be cross about those boys trespassing on Mr Lockwood's land. She might call the police."

"The police!"

"She might start to wish she'd never had anything to do with children like me."

"*Like you?*"

"Evacuees."

Cecily didn't like the sound of this. It sounded like truth. She clumped past the trees, looking ahead to where the woods ceased and the field began. Soon they would step into that golden-green light. "We won't tell Mama. But we could tell Jeremy and Uncle Peregrine?"

"What if we told them, and they went to the ruins, and the boys weren't there?"

". . .Jeremy would laugh at me."

"Better to be safe than sorry," said May.

Sunshine reached out for them, the shade of the forest fell away. Cecily imagined losing May forever and said, "I think you're right."

ON THE SUBJECT OF BRAVERY

The papers, next day, brought outrageous news. An enemy aeroplane, swooping through the dark like a sheenless creature of the night, had dropped its fearsome cargo upon Buckingham Palace. Fortunately the bomb had landed in the quadrangle and not on a royal head, so the King and the Queen, although shaken, were still whole: but the intention was clear. All around the country, people gathered to be appalled. "It's a disgrace," said Mrs Winter. "What did the King and Queen do to deserve that?"

"No more than anyone else," said Peregrine.

"Will you look at the damage. A dirty great mess. What if the King had been standing right there? He'd be mince meat." The housekeeper made a chunky fist. "I tell you, if they harm that poor mutt of a man, I'll strap on a parachute and drop in for a word with Mr Hitler myself."

"A parachute made by May's mum!" said Cecily. She whipped about to May. "You said bombs wouldn't fall on important people's heads, but look – one fell on the King and the Queen!"

"On their quadrangle," replied May. "Not on their heads."

"Our house doesn't *have* a quadrangle. Poor Daddy!"

"It's ridiculous," Heloise opined from the sofa. "It's insane for the King and Queen to risk their lives this way. They should leave the city and go somewhere safe. What do they think they're proving by staying in London?"

Jeremy turned a white face to her. In the six days since their quarrel, relations between mother and son had not improved. Their feud had lasted so long that Cecily had almost forgotten they'd ever lived any way but uneasily. He said, "They're proving they are no better than everyone else."

Lest there was someone less intelligent than herself in the room, Cecily explained, "If ordinary people – normal people – poor people – are getting bombed, the King and the Queen want to be where they can get bombed too. So it's fair."

Heloise said, "But they *are* better than everyone else, aren't they. They're the King and Queen. And as such, they're targets. Worse, they're making targets of everyone around them. That's not fair at all."

Mrs Winter, who wasn't afraid of Mrs Lockwood, said, "Oh, I think it's a great thing that they've stayed in London. When a person sees the King and Queen suffering just the same as they're suffering, sharing the selfsame peril every day and night, it's going to make a difference. It's going to give a person strength."

"It's going to give a person a hernia," said Heloise. "This country has enough to worry about. They would be doing everyone a favour if they took themselves off to the Highlands somewhere, out of harm's way."

"You're not brave, are you, Mother." Jeremy spoke as if from a height. "All you care about is being safe."

"Is there something wrong with wishing to be safe?"

"There is, when it's other people who are dying so you can be kept that way."

Heloise's mouth became the razor-line that Cecily dreaded. "Do you suggest I – oh, I don't know, commandeer a tank and storm the Reichstag?"

"No. But you could admit it's brave of the King and Queen to stay with the people who don't have the luxury of escaping to the countryside."

Heloise's fingers skimmed the fine upholstery of the sofa: May, watching, thought of spiders and webs and elegant spider-legs. "I'm worried about your education, Jeremy." Heloise's voice was the spider's silk, gossamer but deadly. "Time is slipping by. We must get you back into a classroom before your mind turns to porridge. Already you're forgetting your manners. A boarding school would be best, I think. I shall write to your father this afternoon. I'm sure he'll agree, once I tell him my concerns, that you should be sent off immediately to somewhere *very* safe, *very* far away."

Jeremy did not protest or ask forgiveness: his majestic pride, learned at his mother's knee, would not let him, and perhaps he was not sorry. But when the gathering broke up and the family went its separate ways, Cecily, running upstairs to fetch her coloured pencils, found her brother on the first-floor landing, his hands across his face. "Jem?" she said, surprised to see him there, thin and still as a second hand fallen from a clock. "Go away," he said from behind his fingers, and his sister caught her breath: "Oh Jem, are you crying?"

In common with most siblings, Jeremy and Cecily Lockwood had a thousand grievances against one another. But, again in common, for one to realize the other was hurt roused a lion-like concern and sympathy. "Go away!" Jeremy said again, but Cecily would never leave him there, waylaid so wretchedly in this lonely place, the first-floor landing. "What's the matter?" she had to know.

Despair had overtaken him so thoroughly that he couldn't make the traditional denial of anything being wrong. He wiped his face but the tears kept dropping as they will when a heart has received a deep wound. He stormed in a circle, trying but unable to make himself disappear, then stood still, bent with defeat. "Mother doesn't have to *threaten*

176

me," he croaked. "She doesn't have to – send me away. I'm just trying to – *understand* things."

"Oh!" Cecily said, and didn't know what more to say to a boy who was being punished so vengefully for the crime of growing up. "She probably didn't mean it, Jem – you know what Mama's like. She gets cross and says things she doesn't mean. She says things like that to me all the time! *I'm having your hair cut short, Cecily. No more cake for you ever, Cecily.* She'll forget all about it tomorrow, you'll see. And if she still wants to send someone away then, well – she can send me. I won't mind."

In fact to be sent off to boarding school was the most ghastly fate Cecily could imagine, but her brother didn't notice the sacrifice. He wiped and wiped at the tears that would not stop flowing, turned his face to the wall because his legs were too leaden to carry him somewhere he could be alone. The black pool of suffering inside him soaked his voice and words.

"It's not that. I don't care about that. She can say what she likes about sending me away – she can *do* it, for all I care. I might as well be somewhere else. I'm useless here. All I can do here is – watch, and – I'm so worried—"

"Don't be worried." Cecily brushed her brother's sleeve. "You don't need to worry—"

"I do! We all do! They're bombing Buckingham Palace, Cecily! In a few weeks they'll be walking London's streets!"

"No. . ."

"Yes! Read the papers! We're losing this war! We don't have enough soldiers, we don't have good aeroplanes, they're not *afraid* of us! We need to *fight*, but we aren't fighting! We're not going to win! And when we lose, it will be bad. This isn't a game between kids. Everything will change. Our whole lives will change. Everything good will disappear and never come back. They hate us. And they're going to win."

Agony radiated off him – the agony of being insignificant, the agony of a child's fears. He was terrified, and his mother had turned against him, and the warm future he had been taught to expect was melting away like snow. Desperate to comfort him, Cecily said, "We won't lose, Jem. Remember what Uncle Peregrine said: *They can only beat us when we let them.* And we're not going to let them. Daddy is not going to let them—"

"Daddy!" Her brother, slumped against a wall, gave a sickly laugh. "You have so much faith in *Daddy*."

"He always does what he says he will, that's why."

"He can't do everything. He's only a man."

"But that's what they are too, isn't it? Those soldiers in the newspapers. They're just men. Not better or stronger or cleverer men. Not braver than Daddy. Not braver than you."

"Brave!" Jeremy hit the wall with a fist, startling his sister. "Who knows if I'm brave? How brave have I ever been allowed to be?"

"*I* know you're brave!" she hastened. "I know you're very brave! You read all those books and study those hard subjects – that's brave. You learned the piano – that was brave. You play chess with Daddy, and that's brave. And you know what else you do that's brave?"

Her brother stared grimly at nothing. "I don't mean that. You don't understand. Go away and play, Cecily."

She persisted. "You know what's the bravest thing that you do?"

"What?"

"You answer back to Mama."

He smiled reluctantly. "Mama," he said. "Mama thinks I'm ridiculous. That's what she called me, in front of Uncle Peregrine: *infantile*. That means ridiculous."

Cecily lifted her shoulders, let them drop. Momentarily she wished her mother were here, to see the sad thing that she'd done. "You're not ridiculous, Jem," she said. "Mama only said that because she's worried about the war."

"Mother's worried about the war, so she has to be cruel to me?"

"Sometimes she's like that."

The siblings thought on it, a mother whose angry fear landed, wasplike, on the most convenient surface. "She doesn't think you're ridiculous." Cecily came cautiously nearer. "But you know what? She's scared of you."

"*Scared* of me? Why?"

"Because. . ." Cecily didn't quite know how to put it. "Because you're not going to be the person she wants you to be."

If her words had been diamonds, her brother could not have considered them more closely. He said, "I hope I am going to be a good person. I would like to be a good person. Not famous, or remarkable, but. . . True. Loyal. Brave."

"You *are* brave. Brave enough to kill a man!"

Jeremy's fine face, already drained, paled further on being reminded of these words. "I wouldn't want to do that," he said scratchily, "but I would, if I had to. That's what life is, I think: doing what you have to do. Isn't it?"

Cecily looked at him, her fierce tormented brother who urged ruthlessness but couldn't harm a butterfly. She, Cecily Lockwood, believed herself capable of almost anything – if she had to, she would throw a grenade, man a machinegun, strangle an enemy with her bare hands. But Jeremy was different. He was burdened by his decency. Nonetheless she said, "I think so."

He looked away, his eyes wet but the tears stopped, as fragile as one recovering from a depleting illness. The silent Hall stood around them, the staircase with its wide polished treads, the ivory-white passage with its doors and paintings, the intricately patterned powder-pink tiles at their feet. Nothing moved but for a rose in a vase, past its best, which dropped a lank petal. The closeness they'd shared in the last minutes passed like a smile, and awkwardness filled its place. It is a dreadful thing for a boy to be seen weeping by his baby sister. Jeremy tried to pretend it had never happened. He asked, "What are you and May doing today?"

"Nothing. Drawing and colouring. You can do some too, if you like."

It was a wrong, embarrassing thing to say to a young man with a tear-stained face; it made him bad-tempered with her. "Don't be late for lunch," he said nonsensically, for Cecily had never been guilty of that crime; and pushed off from the wall and strode away.

Cecily collected her pencils from her room and on her way back through the house made a detour to the library, where Peregrine was working at his desk. He looked up briefly, said, "May I help you?"

She gripped the pencil-tin for security – the library was an intimidating place when its owner was in residence. The books and bones seemed aloof, the woman in the silver frame unfriendly. "Uncle Peregrine," Cecily said shyly, "if you are staying home today, would you tell us some of the Duke's story after lunch?"

"After dinner. That is the law."

"I would prefer after lunch."

Peregrine's swift writing did not slow, but an eyebrow rose like a hackle. "You'd *prefer* it. Why is that?"

"Because otherwise Mama and Jeremy will talk about the war."

Whatever Peregrine was writing with a beautiful fountain pen was evidently important, and not to be delayed; he kept writing. But he smiled cheerlessly at the paper, a smile meant for her. "All right. After lunch. Now out you go."

His niece took a step backwards to the door. She glanced at the books on the shelves, and at the bones. Then she asked, "Did you ever want to kill a man when you were young, Uncle Peregrine?"

He stopped writing, lifted his gaze. "No."

"But you would, if you had to?"

Peregrine looked at his letter, as if he'd written answers there. After a pause he said, "You know this is not the first world war our country has fought, don't you? You know there was another – the Great War – that was fought before this one? Long before you were born, but not so long ago."

"Yes, I know."

"I was just old enough to fight in that war. I could never be a soldier, though, because of my legs."

The subject of Peregrine's lameness was one she'd been taught never to venture near, and Cecily was aghast to have accidentally strayed into it. She blinked and nodded dumbly.

"A lot of my friends signed up as soldiers at the start of the Great War," her uncle continued. "We'd never lived through a war, so we didn't know what war was like. We thought it would be an adventure. I was envious of my friends who were able to go on this adventure. Later, of course, we realized the truth: that war is almost the opposite to an adventure, that it is a kind of torturous test man craves to put himself through. Part of that test is facing the decision to kill a man, or to let him kill you."

Cecily's voice was a whisper. "If you'd been there, what would you have done?"

"I would kill a man who would otherwise kill me. Of course I would. He would be my utter enemy, that man. This is life, Cecily."

". . . And you'd be proud, if you killed him?"

"*Proud* is not what I'd call it."

Cecily nodded. Words were sticking in her mouth like toffee, but she chewed them out. "Do you think it's brave to *want* to kill an enemy? Do you think it's . . . good?"

"I think it's natural," said Peregrine.

"Huh," said Cecily.

Her uncle waited. "Anything else?"

"I don't think so."

He didn't look down at his papers. "Then off you go."

FROM VILLAIN TO KING

Peregrine declared that if the story was to be told in the middle of the day then the curtains must be closed, the summer light turned away. "We cannot have sunshine on the story," he said. "It's a story for the dark."

"Is the story going to become frightening now?"

"You don't think it's been frightening so far?"

"No," said his niece. "Just wicked."

"I think it's been frightening." Peregrine propped his feet on a sway-backed stool. "It is always frightening to see what power can do. But now, perhaps, the story will become scary even for a dauntless child such as yourself."

"Pfff! I'm not scared of something that happened hundreds of years ago."

"Ah, but this tale reaches across the centuries, into today.

184

If this story hadn't happened, it wouldn't be *our* King and Queen cleaning up after the bomb, but two completely different people. If this story hadn't happened, *our* King and Queen might be running a pet store. Don't think history doesn't touch you, Cecily. The past lives everywhere."

May said, "I don't think the story can hurt us, though. I think it's a sad story, mostly."

"As usual, May, you are correct. In its way it's a sad story, mostly."

Peregrine stirred his tea, set the spoon aside. The afternoon stretched ahead of them, the mantel clock ticking, birdsong tilting in the air. Somewhere men loaded bombs into aeroplanes, somewhere women deciphered a code; somewhere a man stood by a table on which was speared a vast map of the world. But at Heron Hall they settled into their places on rugs and chairs, tea and biscuits at their elbows, a curtain swelling on the incoming breeze; and the dog, sprawled over the floor, sighed with satisfaction.

"The young prince, Edward, is living in the Tower, along with his younger brother, Richard. They've been put there by their uncle, the Duke, supposedly for their safekeeping until the day Edward is crowned. The Duke's seizure of the princes has broken the might of the Queen, and left the Duke with a choice. He can let the future unfold as it should – crown Edward, who hates him, and live, doubtlessly briefly, with whatever happens next – or do what is necessary to bend

185

the future to his will. To a man like the Duke, steeped in ambition from the cradle, it is no decision at all.

"He moves the boys deep into the Tower, into one of its oldest arms, the Keep. The rooms here were handsome, as befits a pair of royal brothers; but the Keep had been built to house high-ranking prisoners, so the rooms were also difficult to reach, and hidden from view. The walls were impossible to chisel away, break down, or climb from. On the windows, there were bars. The boys were still princes, but mostly they were prisoners.

"Some reports claim the boys played in the gardens in the days after Richard joined his brother. Let us hope those reports are true, because it's good to think the children had spirit enough to play. Though only twelve years old, Edward was no fool. He knew his situation was bad. But Richard was a merry lad, and his company surely brightened the sorry existence of his brother. If they did play outside, they must have laughed sometimes, and felt the sun, and seen the birds, and smelt the breeze."

"What would they have played?" Cecily asked, as if considering joining in.

"You're a child: you tell me," said Peregrine.

"Hide-and-seek? Chasey? Climbing trees?"

"Climbing trees? Is that a pastime for kings? Do you think a little prince knows how to climb a tree?"

Cecily pouted. "Maybe he didn't, when he lived in palaces with servants and carriages. But maybe he does now, now they're alone like two mice."

"Well, whether they climbed trees or wandered demurely, their time in the sun would not last. As the days went by, the boys were seen outside less often; and soon they weren't seen at all."

"Dead?"

"Shush!" Jeremy snapped it so crossly that Byron woke alarmed. "Just listen, can't you?"

Peregrine reached for the teapot. "Now, back to our Duke. He'd taken to parading through the streets in the fine clothes of a regent, and his attitude had likewise become haughty. People grew suspicious, and rumours flew as to what this Duke was scheming. Preparations for the Prince's coronation were continuing, but the Duke's army was everywhere in the city, threatening and glaring, and the atmosphere was tense.

"The day of the coronation dawned. Crowds filled the streets. They were waiting to see the Prince, dressed in gold and crimson, crowned as their new sovereign. But the Prince did not appear. Instead, the Duke made a startling announcement. He said that none of the King's children were royal – no, not even Princess Cecily – because the King wasn't supposed to have married the Queen. He'd promised to marry a different lady, someone much nicer than the Queen. But because he had broken this promise and married the Queen instead, none of his children had a right to the throne."

"Good gracious," said Heloise, "that all sounds strange."

"They were strange times, with strange rules. In those

187

days, a promise to marry somebody was as serious as actually being married to them."

Cecily twisted to see her mother. "Imagine if Daddy had promised to marry someone who wasn't you, Mama. Ha! Maybe he did!"

"But was it true?" asked Jeremy. "Had the King really promised to marry a different lady?"

"We don't know every single detail of what the King said and did; but we do know that, in the quest for power, truth is always the first thing left behind. Most people doubted the King had promised to marry another, but the Duke chopped the heads off a few people who said so aloud, and after that nobody argued. The King was dead, crazy Clarence was dead, the princes supposedly weren't royal, and the Duke was the only person left standing to claim the crown. He made a show of refusing it; his friends begged him to reconsider; he reconsidered and agreed. On a tide of lies and disloyalty, the Duke had become King."

"It doesn't matter." Cecily spoke with certainty. "Nothing good is going to happen to him. Bad people aren't happy."

Her uncle pondered this. "Perhaps you're right. Wickedness often wears fancy clothes, dines on rich food, has money, controls armies, rules nations . . . but it never seems to know *joy*. Peace, laughter, trust, ease: these things flee from wickedness like sparrows from the shadow of a hawk. The Duke – I think we shall continue to call him Duke, although he is now the King – was a very learned man. He was interested in art, architecture, music. He read a lot, prayed every day, thought about things deeply. He was, in short, no wooden dolt, no thick-skinned ignoramus. Such a man knows when he is lying. He can be ashamed of himself. I wonder if he lay awake at night, listening to the silence around him. He had kept himself alive. He had sated his ambition for the crown. Once king, he set about improving the country. He passed laws which helped the poorest and most forgotten people. He gave money where it was needed, brought order to where there'd been none. He supported the arts and places of learning. He was, in many ways, a good ruler, and certainly no worse than most others. But the people no longer liked him, and I wonder if such a man, in the depths of night, could like himself.

"Somewhere in the Tower were two boys, prickles buried in the Duke's palm. He could touch nothing without feeling some pain. By the time the Duke was crowned king, the Prince had been in the Tower for almost two months, his small brother for about three weeks. People were starting to wonder about them – to fear for them. Rightful kings had been done away with before: years ago, the Duke himself had something to do with the death of the old sick king, remember?

"But we know things that most people, back then, didn't know: enough scraps survive to prove the princes lived on in their luxurious prison. They had each other for company, and they had four attendants, men specially chosen by the Duke, to act as both servants and gaolers."

The pot was passed around, cups topped up with tea. Cecily smoothed Byron's black coat, Heloise picked dog hair off her skirt. There was one biscuit remaining; Jeremy snapped it and gave the Newfoundland half.

"The Duke now set about being a king," the storyteller continued. "He travelled the country showing off, spending money and being pleasant to everyone; but grouching followed wherever he went. Nobody believed the tale he'd told in order to claim the crown. People wanted the Prince as their sovereign, not this usurping cat-faced Duke. Conspirators began gathering secretly, plotting to rescue the princes and overthrow this false king. Some of their conspiracies were serious and clever, worrying to the Duke. It made him realize – although perhaps he'd always known – that the crown would never sit securely on his head while the princes lived in that Tower.

"All this travelling and uncovering of conspiracies and fretting about the security of his crown took the Duke some time, almost a couple of months. The boys, during these months, stayed in the Tower with their guards, cooped up between the unbreakable walls of the Keep. Their rooms were lushly decorated, but no doubt they were also dark and cold and draughty, being ancient and built from stone. Some say that the Prince, never the most healthy of lads, became sicker, and sunk in misery to the point where he could not, or would not, rise from bed. Perhaps this is true. We know the Prince was smart – smart enough to be afraid. But we also know he was a kind and courageous boy, very aware he was the son of a king, and I wonder if he wouldn't have stayed brave for the benefit of his young brother. I wonder if, even as sorrow wore at him and fear made his heart hammer, he put a smile on his face and found things to laugh about, and joked and played to keep his brother's spirits lively: noble work, fit for a king."

Cecily said, "They couldn't climb trees in the Keep."

"Certainly not," Peregrine agreed. "What do you do when it's raining or you're ill, and you can't go outdoors?"

"I change the clothes on my dolls. The princes wouldn't have done that."

"No, although maybe they had toys, wooden soldiers and skittles and whatnot. Maybe the Prince read to his brother, or invented stories for him. Maybe, if the Prince felt well enough, they raced each other along the passages, or up and down the stairs. Maybe they played the games that boys play today, pretending to be soldiers and sailors."

For the first time since the storytelling began, May made a sound. "Oh!" she said, very quietly, but loud enough to be heard. The family had almost forgotten her, and looked up with surprise. "Army and warships?" the girl asked.

"Why not? The princes, like their uncle, had grown up in a combative world: soldiering and sailing were things they knew. They might have made swords from fire-pokers and horses from straw brooms. They might have draped tables with blankets, and these could have become their boats. Can't

191

you imagine it, the sour old Tower echoing with the shouts of two rough-and-tumble boys? The beds would be in disarray because they'd fought on them like pirates. Feathers would be strewn about because the pillows had been swung as weapons. Can't you picture the princes charging down a corridor, brooms as horses, silk pillowcases as flags? Probably they cornered each other, captured each other, skewered each other and fell down dead and laughing. Can't you see it, May?"

May said softly, "I can."

Peregrine smiled; he reached for the pot but the tea was almost gone. Heloise made to ring for more, but Peregrine said, "Don't bother on my account. We're almost done."

"Almost done?" Cecily was scandalized. "This story isn't scary, Uncle Peregrine!"

He turned his black gaze on to her. "You're not scared?"

"Not by boys playing with broom-horses!"

"Not by the thought of an uncle who kidnaps children and locks them in a dungeon?"

"No!"

"Not by the thought of rooms that had never known sunlight, not since the last stone had been put in place a hundred years before? No sounds of life had passed through those walls for a century – no bird's chirp, no baby's cry, no rattle of passing carts. The prison would have been as silent as a grave. And that's surely what captivity felt like, for two young boys: a suffocating, lonely, living death, trapped in a beautiful tomb. They must have known they were prickles in the palm of their uncle, and that such a man wouldn't tolerate the irritation for long. Maybe they laughed, and told each other stories, and dreamed of being free: but underneath their laughter must have simmered a tortured dread. Every footstep, every turn of a key, would have made their blood run cold. Each time the door opened they'd have hoped to see their mother, the Queen; but she was never there. Instead it would be one of the thickset, silent men who were their gaolers. And every night they must have gone to sleep wondering if they'd live to see morning; if they'd live to grow old."

Cecily stuck out her lip. The storyteller waited for her comment; she had none.

"The Duke was still off parading, far from the city – far enough away to look innocent, should he need to look that way. The prickles in his palm burned at his mind. As long as the princes existed in the Tower, the people would never quieten down and accept him as king. Something had to be done.

"He sent for a man he trusted, a man who slept on the floor like a dog, an unnoticed man in whose brain turned that desperate worm, the desire for power. The desire to sleep somewhere better than the floor; the desire to have a king's gratitude. To earn these, the dog-man would do anything. When the Duke whispered into the man's ear – whispered to the worm, which listened closely – and told him what he required, the dog-man heard, and did not blink.

"Having whispered the words, the Duke headed north, further from the city and the black Tower, to the wild lands where he was still welcome.

"The dog-man took a helper, and rode into the city. In his cloak was a letter from the Duke. He arrived at the Tower in the grey light of evening, gave the letter to the princes' guards. The letter was read and, according to its instructions, the keys to the Keep were handed over to the dog-man. With a growl, the dog-man then sent three of the princes' guards away, keeping one as a second helper in what was to follow.

"Midnight is the time when dark deeds are done: at midnight the dog-man unlocked the door of the room where the two boys slept. No moonlight could have found its way through the walls to shine on their childish faces: whatever light there was would have come from torches, red flames licking the stone. It was a late hour for two children, and no doubt they were asleep; but Edward was unwell and nervous, and maybe he woke at the slightest sound. Maybe he saw a silhouette in the doorway, and knew that this thing he had been waiting for had finally come for him. His brother, huddled in sheets beside him, probably did not stir. Perhaps Edward, remembering he was a prince, imperiously demanded to know what was happening. Possibly the dog-man, like all good dogs, assured him of his kind intent. Or perhaps the three curs went about their work in silence, as befitting those who'd always lived in shadows.

"Two boys, powerless, defenceless, weakened by the

weight of fear, present no difficult challenge to such shadow-creatures. It is a simple thing, the work of mere moments, to cover children's mouths, to swathe them in linen, to lift them from where they lie. When the dog-man and his companions left the room, each helper carried in his arms a bundle wrapped in sheets; and they left behind nothing living but a stray beetle or two, nothing moving but the quaking torch flames. An empty room, and silence; and moonbeams no longer trying to breach the stony walls."

Heloise, Jeremy and May stared at the floor, at the forest of chair legs and the overlapping layers of rug. May's face was white.

"I don't understand." Cecily spoke in a voice which suggested she was about to burst into stinging tears. "Tell me properly what happened. Did they carry them outside to set them free? Is that what happened?"

"Nothing was left living but a stray beetle," her uncle repeated sharply; he looked to the fireplace in which were heaped the black ashes and coals of another day's fire. "That's enough for today," he said. "Go away now, I'm tired."

THREE BOYS DISAPPEAR

May was hurrying; Cecily could hardly keep up. Already they were almost to the woods and Heron Hall had shrunk to the size of a toy behind them. The evacuee had said barely a word since the storytelling had come to an end. Heloise had swept the girls off the floor and out of the room; Jeremy had followed in silence. Peregrine continued to sit in the armchair, his eyes on Byron, the only soul permitted to stay. Cecily had felt hot and disjointed, as if the tale of the princes had given her a dose of flu. May had slipped away without inviting Cecily to follow; but Cecily did follow, as if on a string, stumbling along unwillingly but also irresistibly. They'd left the cobbled yard behind before she'd gathered the wit to say, "May?" They'd crossed most of the wind-tossed field before May answered, "What?"

But by then Cecily had forgotten the question, and was blowing with the effort of hauling herself through the grass. May flitted into the woods and Cecily lurched after her. She knew where they were going and felt increasingly reluctant to arrive, but the string towed her remorselessly. She didn't want to go to the ruins, and May was clearly willing to go alone; but on and on she shambled, as if what must happen could not happen unless Cecily, too, was there.

They crossed the far field and forded the river, stones plunking into the water as they clawed their way up the bank. And finally in front of them, sunk heavily in the land, stood the remains of Snow Castle, and May came to a halt. Her thin chest was heaving, there was dirt on her knees. She drew a breath and shouted, "Hello!"

Hello! replied the castle. *Hell-o.*

"We're here! We've come to see you! Can you see us?"

Us? asked the castle. *Us?*

May's sapphire eyes, alert as a tiger's, searched the edifice. The walls with their glassless windows seemed to stare back sightlessly. "Can you see them, Cecily?"

The breeze leapt up to blow Cecily's blond curls across her face. She wiped them away and they returned eagerly, smothering as seaweed. She scanned the ruins and couldn't see anything but smutted stone and smudged sky. In truth she didn't want to see anything more, and said, "They're not here. They've probably gone."

May said, "No, they're here."

The wind vaulted the river with sudden ferocity. It gushed past the children, unravelled the ribbon in Cecily's hair. It battered the castle like an invading force of old. The castle stood unflinching, impervious to everything but time. The gale moved on, dragging leaves in its wake.

May said, "They played army and warships."

Cecily squinted at the ruins, the ribbon fluttering at her face. She looked high, to where the ceiling would have been; now there was nothing but a hazardous ridge of stones. No child could ever perch there. Only ravens and gargoyles could perch there. She stopped looking there. "It's a coincidence." The breeze took her words. "Any boys would play those games. They always play those games. They think it's fun."

It was a plain fact: boys have played war games for centuries, as if war is fun. May turned her face away. "Hello!" she called, and the castle returned the greeting with unfriendly cheek: *Hello! Oh, hello!*

Cecily tried something: she laughed. It was a fake and empty laugh, but it made May look at her. "It's just an old story, May. It's hundreds of years old." And although she'd been told by her most trusted uncle that history lives forever and touches everything, she said, "That story is just . . . dust. It's not real any more. And there's no such thing as. . ."

She stopped before she said the word. She didn't want to use the word, which was one her daddy would chuckle at. That word only appeared in make-believe, and this was real life. And if, on the odd chance, it *was* true and such things *did* exist in real life – well then, she'd rather not be here. She'd rather be somewhere else. She shifted her weight, started again. "Even if they *were* . . . why would they be *here*? What's Snow Castle got to do with them? It's not in their story."

May gazed at her intently, her eyes shining with a steady light. "But it must be in the story. The castle is the reason Mr Lockwood is *telling* the story, remember?"

Cecily winced. "Maybe it's in the Duke's story, or the Queen's. The princes died – didn't they? – the dog-man came and killed them, didn't he? – and they never had anything to do with Snow Castle."

May stood, buffeted by the breeze; and even as Cecily watched, the light in her eyes faded as if she was recalling what could and couldn't be. She turned to the ruins, said, "I suppose so."

"Think about it!" Cecily clung to her piece of driftwood logic. "This place wasn't in their story, so why would they be here? They wouldn't."

"Hmm," said May.

"They're just two boys, those boys – that's all. Two boys like we're two girls."

"Hmm," said May.

Again they looked into the ruins. Still no bird cried, no dragonfly flew. Cecily looked at the sky, the castle, at the scuffed earth at her feet. It had been a strange long day, cluttered with pictures: a palace courtyard bombed to pieces, her brother weeping on a first-floor landing, her uncle glancing up from his letter, two bundles lying laxly in workmen's arms. She had the dreamy sensation of being feverish, being encased in a skin of glass: everything, so far, was happening outside the glass and could not touch her. But glass is breakable, and Cecily knew that the moment it broke, a river of fear would gush in – fear for her father in the pummelled city, fear for her brother and his troubled heart, fear for the world she would grow up in. She tried to see again what she'd remembered here before, the long-lost toys, the cuddles from her mother, a taste of biscuits: and none of it returned. "Let's go," she said, because she wanted to be far from this trammelled place, she'd suddenly had more than enough of it. "I'm glad they're not here. I don't like those boys. They should stay with their host family and behave themselves. We should have told Mama about them, like I wanted to."

"Don't," said May.

"I won't," Cecily answered curtly.

She had the smallest concern that May wouldn't follow, but the girl turned and traipsed home beside her. Cecily wanted her skin of glass to last as long as possible, so she didn't say much. She pointed out a flock of sheep, a bramble bush, a few other interesting things. They didn't speak of Snow Castle, nor of the princes and the Duke, nor of the look that had come to Peregrine's face at the end of the story, a shadow of hard disgust. And Cecily didn't think to ask why May, who, though brave, was just a little girl, would be so eager, even desperate, to talk to a pair of ghosts.

By the time the family gathered for dinner, the world was normal again. Rain was falling, which was typical, Heloise and Peregrine spoke, as was their habit, as though they'd only recently met, and Jeremy asked his uncle questions about the land. It was almost as if the war wasn't happening, until Heloise spoiled it. "I suppose it will be another long night in London," she said. "I expect the aeroplanes will come again tonight."

It was Cecily's favourite dessert, strawberry tart, and she didn't appreciate having a bomb dropped on it. She put her fork down and sighed. "I assume so," Peregrine said.

"And once again we'll be able to do simply nothing to prevent it?"

"That's likely," Peregrine agreed.

"We're so fortunate to be here," Heloise said; and shivered at some memory of having come within a whisker of actually not being there. "Aren't we, children?"

"Yes," said May and Cecily, but Jeremy only glanced at his uncle, and in that glance there was certainly gratitude, but something else besides: a barely quelled impatience with such sentiments, which he would not tolerate any more.

And maybe it was this glance that made Peregrine, at breakfast the next morning, look up suddenly from the newspaper and ask, "Where is Jeremy?"

His teacup stood empty, his plate pristine, his chair tucked neatly against the table. At this hour of the morning, the light came through the windows in such a way that the chair and the porcelain looked dipped in gold, heavenly. "He must be asleep," Cecily said, lunging to pluck the best toast from the rack. "More for us!"

Peregrine's gaze swept the room, stopped briefly on May, who was watching him, and moved on. "Run upstairs and find him. His breakfast will go cold."

"But –"

"Now, please."

"Hurgh!" Cecily pushed back her chair.

When she'd left the room and clomped off down the hall, Peregrine looked again at the evacuee. "Have you seen Jem this morning, May?"

"No. I'm sorry." The little girl looked at the table, the bowls, the pots and napkins, the silver cutlery. "Has he gone?" she asked.

The wise lonely man looked at the wise lonely child, and answered honestly. "I suppose he has."

ONE IMPORTANT CHILD

He was gone. He had left, on his dresser, a note which Cecily carried downstairs at a gallop. *I can't stand by and do nothing*, it read. *That is not noble. Please don't worry about me.* Peregrine read the note with a soft smile. "*That is not noble*," he mused.

Heloise, of course, had to be told. She emerged from her room like a wild witch, flew hissing to her son's bedroom. She saw for herself that the room contained no fourteen-year-old boy. She glared again at the note crushed in her hand. It bore no time of writing, but the stillness of the room – the coldness of the grate, the closedness of the curtains, the very thin gap around the wardrobe's slightly-open door – testified he'd been gone for hours. He had waited until night was at its thickest before slipping into the dark. "Find him!"

commanded Heloise; then, more like a mother and less like a witch, moaned, "Jem, you silly boy."

That morning, Heron Hall seemed the roost of flighty birds. The staff went about their chores distractedly, with frequent stoppings to update their understanding of the situation. Cecily, May and Byron found a corner in the kitchen where they could go overlooked while remaining warm, fed and informed.

Within hours of the discovery of the note, certain facts were known. Jeremy had taken his coat, boots and money, as well as a change of underclothes which, carrying no suitcase, he must have stuffed in his pockets. The grounds of Heron Hall had been thoroughly searched by the staff, and no sign of the heir to the house had been found. Hobbs, the Hall's driver, had gone to the village to make enquiries, and returned to report that no young man matching Jeremy's description had bought a ticket or boarded a train. "So he's on foot," said Mrs Winter, leaving the house to keep itself while she sat down for mid-morning tea. "Wandering the road like a tinker."

"The police will pick him up," said Cook with satisfaction, as if the collection would be followed by Jeremy's boiling in a pot.

"The police?" Cecily sat up. "Are the police looking for him?"

"Probably not *looking for* him," said the housekeeper. "Probably got better things to do than hunt for a naughty boy. But probably they'll find him. They'll have to answer to your mother if they don't, and if that isn't a good reason to bring out the bloodhounds and track him even to the ends of the earth, I don't know what is."

Cook smirked. "Good luck to him. Enjoy his freedom while it lasts."

"Isn't freedom he's after. He wants nobility, according to his letter."

"Nobility? What's that? *Nobility*. There's nothing noble in this world any more."

"Wants to make a pest of himself, by the looks of it."

Her brother's escapade had initially astonished and hugely impressed Cecily; now, three hours later and cooling like gruel, it was shaming her. Jeremy had upset Mama and disrupted the house, and now the police were involved, as if he'd committed a grubby crime. She was quite certain he would soon be found and brought home, and then everyone would quietly laugh at him. He had done something foolish. Somehow, he had sullied Heron Hall, or at least the flawless memories she had of it. He'd be brought back and then sent to boarding school, and he had only himself to blame. Cecily was angry. "I agree!" she declared imperiously. "He's making a pest of himself." And looked expectantly at May but the girl was typically unforthcoming, as though her thoughts were rare jewels only she could admire.

By lunchtime Jeremy should have been sitting in his place at the table, but he wasn't. Heloise tried to laugh, as if the situation amused. "I don't know what he thinks he's doing," she said. "What is the point of it? What's he trying to say, Peregrine? You were a boy once: what do you think he wants?" And Peregrine didn't answer beyond smiling a cool smile, because they all knew what Jeremy wanted, even Heloise. He had been telling them since the day they arrived.

Midday dragged into afternoon. Hobbs had been away from the house for hours, driving the roads and laneways that the runaway might travel. Cecily and May played with Cecily's dolls. Cecily did not speak about it, but she was somewhat concerned for her brother now. Evening was coming. The day, which had been mild, was growing damp and overcast.

At five o'clock Heloise decided to telephone her husband to tell him that his wayward son had escaped Heron Hall and was presumably making his way to the city. "It's really very wicked of Jeremy," she said. "Humphrey has enough to worry about." Cecily eavesdropped on the conversation, which took place in an alcove where the telephone sat like a crown in a museum. "You'll tell me the moment he turns up, won't you?" she heard her mother ask, and there was a note of real worry in her voice when she said it, a note she had kept quelled so far.

By dinnertime there was despondency, although Cook had made a special effort to serve up something consoling. The fragrant courses on silver and china, the polished furniture reflecting the dancing fire, the curtains and paintings, the rugs on the floor only highlighted the emptiness of the night outside. Cecily thought it might be nice to talk of something other than Jeremy, if only to make everything, even her brother's absence, seem natural:

but Heloise brushed her attempts aside, her daughter an irritation, her world compressed around the figure of a single boy. "He's going to London, of course," she said, as if she hadn't yet settled this assumption into her head. "If he walks all the way, it will take days. So presumably he won't walk. Presumably a farmer or a lorry driver will pick him up and drive him to the city or to a train station somewhere."

"Presumably," said Peregrine.

"He'll look like a tramp," Cecily envisaged, "all shabby and smelly on the side of the road."

"Oh, don't say that, Cecily. That's not how he'll look at all. Really, that's an absurd thing to say. Do try to think about what comes out of your mouth before it does so, please. Sit and be quiet, or leave the room."

Cecily cowered as if whipped. May looked away from her friend's embarrassment. Heloise had already forgotten her daughter. "I don't know what he thinks he can do in London. Something *noble*, according to his letter. He *can't stand by and do nothing*. He hasn't thought anything through sensibly, of course. No one will want a boy wandering about, getting in the way. He'll be no help to anyone. What can he do that's of use?"

She shook her head many times, as if to shake out the vision of her fine-boned son smeared with soot. Perhaps the image dropped away, only to be replaced by another; something worse. "And London is so fearful at the moment, isn't it. If he's wandering the streets, the lights are out, the aeroplanes are coming, the bombs dropping, there's no shelter close by. . ." She stopped, put a hand to her eyes. "What makes a boy want to do such a thing? What makes men create a world where a boy feels he must do such things?"

May glanced at Peregrine. He looked more like a warlock than ever. He answered with a word: "Power."

Heloise smiled rancorously. "Ah yes, how could I forget. Idiotic power. So precious that a man will extinguish the lives of thousands, *hundreds* of thousands, just so he can hold it in his hands for a while. So precious that the life of a child is nothing to him – absolutely nothing."

Peregrine reached for the carafe, poured the bruise-black wine. Cecily had leaned as far back from the table as her seat would allow. A feeling that everything was crushingly bad had descended upon her. She didn't want to be in the dining room, or in Heron Hall, or in the countryside. She didn't want to be anywhere. If she had the chance to be with her brother, she would not even be there.

Heloise took several sips from her glass. Her blade-edged gaze would not settle, but ran about like a starving rat. She said, "Remember how he spoke that day. *I could kill a man*. As if that's what a mother wants her son to do. It isn't. It never has been. Every man is another mother's son."

"Helly," said Peregrine, which was a name Cecily had never heard him use, a name which made her mother's panicked eyes swing to him and stop there. "You should rest. You're tired."

"I'm not tired, I'm not tired at all. I'll sit up, if you don't mind. I don't want to be asleep when he comes home. Except

208

I don't suppose he'll come home tonight, not now. It's too dark, too late. He'll hole up like a badger somewhere. He's been so cross with me lately, but I've only wanted him to be safe. Now look what he's done. Disappeared into thin air. Hardly *safe*, is it."

"I'm sure he's fine—"

"Are you?"

"What harm can he come to, out there? There's nothing but trees and fields. And he's a clever boy, Heloise. He can look after himself."

"No doubt you're right. He's extremely capable. And he's always been quite – rustic, hasn't he? He'll probably enjoy sleeping in a ditch."

"Indeed. I shouldn't worry."

Heloise smiled quaveringly. She gave her spoon a slight cuff, so it clinked against her bowl. "It's not the ditches which bother me," she admitted. "You'll say I'm being silly, but I can't help feeling – you don't think – you don't think he'd try to – *enlist*, do you, Peregrine?"

Cecily felt the word as a thump to the chest. The idea of her pale, breakable brother signing up and marching on to a battlefield, becoming a soldier not in a game but in real and dreadful life, made her cry out, "Mama!"

"Helly. Be sensible. He's a boy."

"Yes, a boy who wants to fight! Who's been taught that *heroes* fight. As if one boy's death amid tens of thousands isn't hateful and pointless but *heroic*, and, God help me, *noble*. . ."

"Mama!"

Peregrine said, "Jeremy's young. He's clearly a child. If he tried to enlist, they'd simply turn him away."

"Good!" Heloise gave a crumpled laugh. "Let them turn him away! Let them send him packing. He doesn't belong to the country. I won't give him to those bloodthirsty generals and their army, their tanks, their shooting, their bombs. He isn't yours to kill, Peregrine!"

"Mama!" Cecily bawled. "Is Jem going to France? Is he going to die?"

"*No.*" Peregrine said it like a fist coming down. "Nothing will happen to Jeremy. He won't become a soldier. He is just a *child.*"

"Just a child, that's right! And children must be kept safe. We'll pack them on trains and send them off to live with strangers who are good enough to take them in, anything to keep the dear things away from the enemy—"

"Heloise."

"– but we'll also teach them that war is necessary, and that dying for your country, when your whole life is ahead of you, is a good and honourable and glorious thing. And if that's not delivering a child into the hands of the enemy, then I don't know what is. Really, I don't know what is."

She pushed back her chair and rose like a spectre, wan and almost transparent. A churning turmoil had overcome her, visible for all to see: Cecily had never seen her mother so unravelled. "I'll go to my room to wait," she said. "I'm being silly, I know. Of course a bomb won't fall on him. That's a silly thing to think. Of course he can't enlist. They're very fussy about who they'll kill. *Of course* he won't get hurt: such things aren't meant to happen to children, so of course they don't. Bring him home, Peregrine. Promise me you will. It's been a whole day now, and that's long enough."

Stunned, they watched her depart as a wave leaves the shore, drawn away by irresistible forces. She went up the long staircase to her room; and although she would rise the next day and every day for many years to come, Heloise Lockwood was never the same person after that night. She never recovered from the realisation that children are wilful people; she never trusted them again. Worse, she discovered that, when it counted, the world was immune to her wishes and commands. She who'd believed herself important found she was just an angry bee in a jar. She continued to buzz and batter at the glass; but from this night forward she always knew, in her heart, that her buzzing and her battering were nothing more than noise.

When her mother had left the room, Cecily turned a colourless face to her uncle. "No," he told her again.

May was gazing at the door that had closed behind Mrs Lockwood. Eventually she looked at Peregrine. In a voice as meek as a mouse she asked, "Where is he?"

"I don't know," said the man. "Not here. But not where your father is, either."

"All right," said the girl.

That evening, in Heron Hall's windows, lamps burned

211

like wolves' eyes, reaching into the dark to light a path for the missing boy. Somewhere across the chopping Channel, sons fought one another into the night, gunfire flaring orange and white, blood flowing more black than scarlet. In the city, fires burned around buildings that minutes earlier had been solid and standing yet now lay tumbled over the road. Somewhere in the dense sky flew aeroplanes, their stomachs stuffed with bombs; somewhere, underground, ears strained for the sound of these planes, the thrum that would stir a grinding fear. Somewhere, in secure strong rooms, stood those for whom this nightly misery was simply the war going as planned.

But that night, none of this mattered to the occupants of Heron Hall. All was insignificant compared to the loss of one important boy.

Morning saw Cecily hurrying along the first-floor passageway. She found his bedroom silent, an abandoned sanctuary. His bedclothes were still smooth, as he'd left them, the pillows like bales of snow. She looked at the small things her brother owned, a tortoiseshell hairbrush, a very-read book, a spoon, tortured with corrosion, that he'd dug up from the ground. He never liked her to touch his belongings and she didn't do so now, as if obeying his rules somehow meant he was near. "Jeremy Joseph Lockwood," she said, closing her eyes and trying to envisage, by mystic magic, exactly where he might be; but all she saw was a memory of him standing, weeping, on the landing, and all she felt was a swilling resentment for her mother. *Infantile*, Mama had called him, meaning he was ridiculous, shaming him before Uncle Peregrine, making him determined to prove his courage. If Mama hadn't done that, Jem would still be here. Heloise was most upset that he was gone, yet with her the blame lay squarely . . . but Cecily was only twelve years old, and still needed to forgive the faults of her mother. She looked for someone else to blame.

For a second morning Jeremy's place at the breakfast table was empty, although the maid had laid out a setting of plate, bowl, cutlery, napkin and cup, in case, Cecily supposed, he returned suddenly and starving. May eyed the vacant chair in silence. "He's not home," Cecily informed her breakfast companions.

"Not yet," said Peregrine.

"Will we find him today?"

"I hope so. But perhaps not."

"If he's going to London, will he get there today?"

Peregrine took toast from the rack, carved a wafer of butter. "You ask me questions as if I know the answers, Cecily."

"Well, usually you do."

There was a rough tone in her voice which both May and Peregrine noticed but neither commented on. She snatched some toast and buttered it so severely that the slice cracked like an ice floe. She saw, again, her brother in tears on the first-floor landing. Words came to her that she'd forgotten: *I would like to be true. Loyal. Brave.* It was sad that he expected such grand things from himself when he was merely a boy. Bluntly she said, "I think Mama is right. Jeremy's run away to join the army. He's going to go to France and get shot. An enemy will shoot him and they'll be happy about doing it, just like you said, Uncle Peregrine."

"That won't happen," said May.

"Oh, how do *you* know?" Cecily wheeled as if this was the opportunity she'd been waiting for. "Just because your dad is a soldier and your mum's making parachutes, you think you know everything. It's *your* fault Jem's run away!"

The child, startled, shrank in her chair. Peregrine asked, "Why exactly is it May's fault?"

"She's always showing off, that's why! Showing off about her dad being a soldier and her mum making parachutes!"

"I don't!" protested May.

"Yes you do! *It's better than doing nothing,* you said, as if *we're* doing *nothing* and *you're* doing everything. Even though my daddy is important in the war, and your dad is just a teacher! You made Jeremy be ashamed and run away. If he gets killed, it will be your fault. I wish you'd never come here, May! I wish I had left you in the town hall. You're just like everyone said you'd be, a *troublemaker*. I'd rather have Jeremy here, not you!"

May, white as death, said nothing. Peregrine gazed at his niece. "I don't think your brother would be pleased by your saying that," he said.

Cecily barked, "I don't care!" And, as if shot out by cannons, two tears leapt from her, splattering her plate. "Aarg!" she wailed. "Argh! Ahargh!"

May looked to Peregrine. "I want to go home."

"No, you can't!" Two more tears banged like bullets on to the table before the flow found its natural path down Cecily's cheeks. "You're not allowed! You have to stay here! No one else is allowed to leave!"

She folded her hands across her face and wept dramatically. Neither Peregrine nor May moved to console her. "I want to go home," whispered May.

Peregrine turned to her. "I hope you won't. Not yet."

"I don't want you to go!" Cecily bawled behind her hands. "I want Jem to come home!"

"She blames me," said May.

"She doesn't. She's frightened and confused. May," said Peregrine, "I know these past weeks have been hard for you. I know what you've been through, and what you've lost. Nothing can change the past; and if you really want to go home, of course you can. But you are an important guest here, perhaps the most important guest the Hall has ever hosted. I hope you will stay. I would hate to see you leave before I know that where you're going is somewhere you'll be safe. I would not like to lose you."

May only looked at him, very little and imploring, unable to lift the heavy words she might have said in reply: *I miss my mother, I need my father* weigh too much for a child. Cecily, realising she had stopped being the centre of attention of her audience, screamed, throwing down her hands to reveal streaked cheeks. "I'm *sorry*, May! Why do you even listen to me? I'm horrible, you know that!" And dropped her head so low that her nose snuffled on her toast and her curls floated on her tea. Peregrine and May observed her without sympathy. Cecily grovelled in her plate some moments more, coating her nose in butter, getting jam in an ear. Her face, when she raised it, was a veritable buffet. "You're not allowed to go, May! You have to stay. You can't run away *too!* The *whole world* can't run away!"

May's stare was withering. "I don't have to do what you say."

"Wahk!" shrieked Cecily.

Peregrine sipped his tea and said, "If you must go, May, I hope you'll at least stay to hear the end of the Duke's story."

"There's more?" gagged Cecily.

"Does it have something to do with Snow Castle?" May asked.

"It has something to do with Snow Castle," confirmed Peregrine.

Cecily moaned, "You mustn't tell it until Jem comes home. . ."

Peregrine shrugged. "Jeremy has heard enough. Heloise has heard enough. The end of the story is for you two."

"Don't tell it!" The bigger girl abruptly lurched forward and shouted: as if the evacuee were a fairytale princess who could be freed from captivity by the correct combination of words, she said, "As soon as you tell it, May will go!"

Proud May ignored her cruelly, said, "Please Mr Lockwood, tell it now."

FROM KING TO LEGEND

They did not retire to the brown warmth of the den, but stayed in the breakfast room with the fair light of morning shining on the honey and the backs of their hands. The frostiness between the girls was thawed, slightly, by the summoning of Byron, who begged scraps from them. For a final time the storyteller invited the Duke into the house.

"So our man is finally king," he began, "but nothing is as it should be. Conspiracy and rumours fly about him like locusts. People think only of the princes in the Tower, those boys with the rightful claim to the throne. The Duke reasons he will never truly hold the crown until this matter is dealt with.

"He summons the dog-man. *Loyal dog, if you love your master, do as I command.* And the dog-man takes assistants and goes to the Tower. They climb the stairs to the Keep. They enter the room and see two boys asleep. The dog-man whines his orders. The assistants do as they are told. They press blankets to the faces of the children until there is stillness and silence."

"Murdered them," marvelled May.

Peregrine selected a hard-boiled egg from the bowl. Watched intently by Byron, he cracked and peeled the shell. Then he sliced the egg into wedges, salted the yolk, and offered the pieces to the girls, who shook their heads. "How fortunate you both are," he said, "that you can refuse to eat. . . I don't know what happened that night in the Tower. I wasn't there. Nearly five hundred years have passed since then; that's a long time. And secrets are easily buried, especially by a loyal dog. One thing is certain: after that night, the princes were never seen again. In the Duke's brief reign as king, there were times when it would have been useful for him to pull a live prince from his sleeve: but he never did, probably because he couldn't. And it is certainly true that, at the time, the locusts of rumour began to whisper that the princes were dead."

"Dead! He killed them. And they were only children!"

Peregrine looked at Cecily. "Even in such a violent era, the killing of children was considered a despicable crime. But what crime, in which era, has ever gone uncommitted?"

"But they weren't only *children* – they were his *nephews!*" She glared as if he, an uncle, must answer for the behaviour of all uncles. Peregrine seemed unfazed.

"His nephews, that's so. But would that have made a difference to a man such as the Duke? Remember, he'd said nothing in defence of his brother, Clarence; but Clarence was mad, beyond saving. The princes were a different matter – but the Duke remained the same man. The opinion of the locusts was that the boys were dead. And indeed, the Duke didn't move to quieten the rumours, but rather let them spread – although in his version the princes weren't murdered, obviously, but died of disease. If the Prince and his brother were believed deceased, there could be no more calls to make Edward a king. . .

"But a curious aspect of power is that, like a bull being baited, it must forever be in a fever to guard every flank. One biting, snapping threat is stamped out, only for another to fasten teeth to its rump. The princes were removed, but no one believed the Duke's story that they'd died from disease. Everyone was certain the Duke had had a hand in their demise; and everyone was appalled to have such an unscrupulous man on the throne. And some of these appalled people had been friends of the Duke, but would be friends with him no longer.

"Now we must introduce another character to the stage, the previously unheard-of character who swoops in when all seems lost. We shall call him the Tudor. He is but a twig of the royal family tree, and has a very faint claim to the throne. He has been living abroad, penniless, for years, and no one except his mother much knows or cares about him. But now the Duke's enemies realize the Tudor might be worth dragging in from obscurity. Here was a man who could legitimately wear the crown, were it to be pushed from the Duke's head.

"And that head, according to some observers, was not a happy one after the princes vanished. The Duke, always God-fearing, took to serious prayer. It's said he paced the corridors at night, afraid to sleep and dream."

"Serves him right," said Cecily. "Don't you think so, May?"

May ignored her. "What was the Queen doing all this time?"

"The Queen . . . well, when she hears the rumours that her sons are dead, she does what all mothers, losing sons, must do. She falls to her knees and asks the wind, the rain, the sky, the sun, the moon, the clouds and the stars to take her life instead of theirs. And when this can't happen, she swears revenge against the man she has always hated, and now has reason to hate a thousand times more.

"Thus powerful people align themselves against the Duke. They hasten the spread of the rumour that the princes have died at his command. Anger sizzles over the land. More people join the Tudor conspiracy. They send the Tudor an invitation to invade the country and seize the crown.

"But the Duke is not without a few friends still, and one of them got wind of the uprising. The Duke readied to fight, but for once he didn't have to. As the Tudor prepared to invade, a gale blew, battering the rebel forces to pieces. The Tudor popped back into his hidey-hole before the Duke could grab him; but others were grabbed, and heads rolled. The uprising was hobbled, though not obliterated, as we shall see; and now the Duke knew his peril. He tried, over the next while, to earn back the respect of his subjects, passing sensible laws, caring for the poor, being well-behaved, generous and holy. But no matter what good thing he did, no one would forgive him, and nobody would love him."

"Serves him right," Cecily snarled again.

The maid came to the door. "More tea, Mr Lockwood?"

"Please. Any news?"

"Nothing, Mr Lockwood. Sorry."

Cecily sighed. She looked out the window, into the world where her brother had gone. "At least it's not raining," she observed. Jeremy would probably be quite content tramping the roads in the sunshine, kicking stones, drinking from brooks.

When fresh tea had been brought and steam was whiffling from the cups, the storyteller resumed. "And now something happened which marked the beginning of the end for the Duke. His seven-year-old son, his only child, a boy he loved dearly, suddenly died. Fingers pointed: the boy's death was clearly divine vengeance for the murder of the princes, and maybe even the pious Duke saw things this way. Personally I would rather not believe in a God who would claim the life of a child in retaliation for the death of two others, but these were superstitious, vengeful times. Before a year had passed, the Duke's wife also sickened and died; yet the Duke, in his grief, received little sympathy. In fact, a rumour was loosed claiming he'd poisoned his wife. Almost everywhere he looked now, among high people and low, the Duke found only contempt. Power, which had once appeared so handsome to him, had warped into something barren and foul. Maybe that is what power always does. Maybe that is the nature of the thing.

"The Tudor, meanwhile, had been crouched in his hole, spinning his web of treachery. He'd regrouped his forces and repaired his gale-wrecked ships. When he finally made his move, arriving unannounced on the Duke's shore, the Duke reacted in a surprising way. History says he greeted the news with happiness. Presumably he was pleased that the chance to finish off the pretender had arrived. But perhaps he was happy because—"

"Because he'd given up," said May.

"Because nothing had turned out the way he'd hoped," Peregrine agreed. "Because everything he'd done had been wrong. Because nothing he'd gained had proved worth having. Because he'd lost what he most desired to keep. And now came this conflict, which would be pure and purifying. The Duke knew how to fight and win; but he would also have known he could be defeated, and he was still willing. Here was the chance to finish everything, one way or the other.

"He summoned his army and marched south to meet

222

the Tudor. Arriving at the edge of a field beyond which the enemy was massing, he set up camp and tried to rest. It rained that night, and the Duke slept badly, troubled by nightmares. In the morning he was pale, but he was ready.

"By the end of the battle, which was mercifully brief, the Duke lay dead on the field. He had fought valiantly, as does a true warrior prince. Many of his supporters had deserted him during the clash, swapping sides when it appeared that the Tudor would win. The Duke had survived long enough to see this – to know he'd been abandoned by the last of those he trusted, and now had nothing left to lose but his life. So he charged forward alone, and cut down the enemy's flag, and then was cut down himself, hacked at by a dozen swords."

"Oww," said Cecily.

Peregrine smiled faintly. "He had been king for a whisker over two years; two years haunted by the presence, and absence, of two boys. His body was treated as were the corpses of criminals: he was stripped and kicked, and displayed in rags to the crowd. He was buried without ceremony in a pauper's grave, and years later his bones were dug up and thrown into the river, and that was the very last of him, although his reputation lived on, becoming more and more deformed with time until he came to be seen as a monster. His rival, the Tudor, was crowned the new king, and the people flocked to him, and his twig of the royal tree would grow strongly to this day, so that our King in Buckingham Palace, the one who just missed being flattened by the bomb, might be selling flowers on a street corner if the Duke hadn't died on that field. And the Duke would not have died on the field if he'd been able to prove the princes were alive, for if the princes lived, the Tudor could never have claimed the crown. But that is how life works – something is done, and it is never undone. Everything that changes, changes everything forever. If the Duke hadn't died, this war might not have been declared—"

"And Jem would not have run away."

"Exactly. Jeremy would not have run away."

Cecily let out a sigh. "That was a funny story. Even though the Duke was bad, it was quite sad."

"It's not finished, though." May spoke up anxiously. "You've forgotten something, Mr Lockwood."

"Have I?"

"You've forgotten Snow Castle."

Peregrine smiled again, and they knew he'd done no such thing. "Ah, Snow Castle." He rapped his fingers on the table, leaned back into the sunlight. "Everything I've told you of this story so far has been fact – you can read it in any history book, see paintings of the Duke, the Queen, the Tudor in galleries, see artefacts from their lives in museums. But Snow Castle takes us into the realm of wishes and imaginings. No one knows what the castle looked like when it was new and strong. No one knows the exact truth about its past. Snow Castle stands not in the real world, but in the land of what-could-be."

"That's all right," said Cecily. "I like that land of what-could-be."

"Well, I promised I would tell you the legend of the castle, and I will. Would you be so kind as to pour the tea, Cecily; thank you." He took up the cup, sat back in the sun, vanished in its sparkly light, reappearing again. "When your mother sent you out of London, May, and when your father sent you, Cecily, here to Heron Hall, they sent you north – into the corner of the country where the Duke had felt most secure. He owned houses and land throughout this region, including the house he considered home. His wife and son lived here, and he had friends here even to the end. What peace he found, he found here, in the north. He knew this country like the back of his hand."

Both girls glanced at Peregrine's hands as if there could be seen an engraved map of the Duke's territory.

"Ever since the princes disappeared, there have been those who say the dog-man was sent not to murder the princes that night, but rather to spirit them away to a secret place where they would cause no trouble and never be found. These people argue that, since the princes had been declared not royal, they were no threat to the Duke – certainly not a threat to warrant committing a horrendous crime. They've pointed out that the Duke was not without goodness, and that he was, above all, a man who feared his God – a God who, we can be certain, wouldn't take kindly to the snuffing of innocents. These people ignore the fact that no one believed the princes weren't royal. They overlook the Duke's unease around the time the brothers disappeared. They brush over his history of removal of his rivals, and the fact that the princes disappeared while they were in his care. Most of all, they forget that, even when rumours were hounding him, when the Tudor was scheming against him, when pulling a prince from his sleeve could have changed things in an instant, the Duke never so much as reached for a cuff.

"Those who believe the princes didn't die that night point to the fact that many important children were held in safehouses at that time, usually deep in the country in the custody of wealthy nobles. Here they were cared-for and educated, as well as kept out of the way. Clarence's son lived in such a place; the Queen's daughters were also held, at one time, in a safehouse. It was a pleasant enough way to live, and certainly a child must live *somewhere* . . . but it was, undeniably, a form of imprisonment. Safehouse children were not free.

"So it's said by some that the dog-man carried the blanket-wrapped brothers not to a dank corner where their bones would rot away, but out of the dreadful Tower, out of the sleeping city, out into the countryside riding north, always north, into the land where the Duke felt at home, where he was trusted, where he could claim the friendship of secret-keeping men. Rumour has it that here, in the secluded north, the princes were stashed, left in the care of the dog-man and his helpers, taught, fed, tended, but never allowed to step beyond the walls of the castle. Left to amuse themselves, to remember their mother and father, perhaps to plot boyishly of escaping to London and triumphantly claiming the crown. Left to grow shy, and suspicious of strangers, who'd never shown them much kindness. Left, in the hope that they would fade from memory in this wild, lonely place."

"In Snow Castle."

May barely spoke it. Peregrine hardly nodded. "There were many castles around, some of them hidden and difficult to reach, as is often the nature of castles. Many of them would have been suitable for housing princes. But Snow Castle, with its walls of white marble, must have been a special place – a place of incredible richness completely hidden from the rest of the world. Certainly it seems the kind of place where a grand crime could be committed against history, against truth. Why else would such a glorious building be so ruined now, so rejected, so. . ."

"Disgraced," said May.

He looked at her intently, his eyes black flints. "Disgraced. That is the word." His gaze travelled the room, over the table and the sideboard and the dog sleeping on the floor, and glided back to his listeners. "It is only a legend," he said. "Strange things can happen, but usually they don't. Usually, what happens is the most ordinary thing. That doesn't mean that life is drear. It simply means you can trust it never to fall below expectation; and sometimes, very occasionally, to soar into the realm of the incredible."

He did something, then, that May would never forget: he winked at her as a conjurer on a stage might wink to a child in his audience, as though nobody existed but they two. Then he got to his feet and, followed by his dog, limped from the room, a man who lived, who would live forever, in a house which stood around him like a fortress and a friend, who'd lost his wife and infant so long ago that no one spoke to him about them any more, who lived a life of quiet mystery surrounded by what pieces of it remained.

AN UNDERSTANDING IS
REACHED

The evacuee waited only a moment before jumping from her chair and hurrying from the room. Cecily – yet again as if impelled by some strong string – followed in the child's nimble wake. Again, she knew where May's rush was carrying her. "I don't think we should go there," she fretted. "It's horrible, May." But the girl didn't answer; Cecily might as well not have been there. They reached the mud room and May pulled off her shoes. Her wellingtons were a drab brown colour, not the interesting maroon of Cecily's; she slipped her stockinged feet into them while Cecily watched from the doorway, wringing her fingers. When she was ready May stood up, and looked at Cecily as at a black spider who'd been scurrying in her wake. "Stay here and play with your dolls," she said. "I don't need you to come."

"Oh May, are you cross with me?"

May ducked past, and Cecily, struggling on the string, pursued her. They went out into the courtyard, startling a trio of hens. The day was cooler than it promised, the sun weaker than it had seemed from the breakfast room. May opened the gate and went into the field, and Cecily slogged after her. A flock of birds came up from the grass like arrows shot by Indians; Cecily squeaked in surprise. May only marched on. "You should go back," she stated woodenly. "You haven't got your boots."

Cecily was moving too fast to risk looking at her feet. "Aw well—"

"Go back. Your mother is already angry. You'll get into trouble, and then everything will be worse. Everything is already bad enough without your mother being angry about wet boots!"

"May!" Cecily cowered: she had never heard her friend shout. "Don't be cross at me."

"You blame me for Jeremy running away!"

"Not now I don't, not any more—"

"You said I was showing off about my dad being a soldier, and that's why Jem ran away! And I *never* did that, I *never*—"

"Ug!" Cecily had little air to spare for gasping in dismay. Nonetheless she managed a sound that conveyed repentance and shame, as well as a little impatience. "I said I was sorry, you know I didn't mean it, I say lots of things I don't mean!"

May stopped, so Cecily on her suddenly-slackened

string almost bowled over. "You can't say something, and hurt someone's feelings, and then say you didn't mean it and think that makes it better. It doesn't. Go back, Cecily. I don't need you with me. I'm going to find those boys—"

"No, don't!"

"– and I'm going to ask for their help. So I don't need yours."

"I'm *sorry!*"

"You're only sorry because I'm angry. Otherwise you wouldn't care. You're mean and selfish, and I don't want to be your friend. You made me want to go home, and I can't go home."

"May, I'm *truly* sorry—"

"You might be worried about Jem, but you're not the only one worried, Cecily. You're not the only one who's lost somebody."

Cecily had never felt so crushed and vile. She actually thought she might be sick. She scrambled to keep up as the girl marched away. "I know it's not your fault that Jem's gone."

"It's too late," said May.

Cecily felt sicker, but pressed on. "It was Jem who said we should take an evacuee, did you know? That day at the town hall. He probably would have run off sooner, if you hadn't been here."

May said nothing to these words like pretty baubles on a burnt Christmas tree. Cecily, her heart sunk as low as it could go, bumbled on.

231

"If Jem hadn't said we should take you, then we wouldn't be here in the meadow. Isn't that funny, May? It's exactly what Uncle Peregrine said: one change, changes everything."

A frown swooped on to May's brow and hovered there, vulture-like; it did not fly away. The field delivered the pair into the shadows of the woods: birds scattered, although not the one with its wings spread across May's face. Cecily cast furtive glances at her. The girl might have been thinking anything. Unable to compose other ways of apologising, Cecily fell silent, moving hangdog between the trees.

They could see the sun nosing at the brackeny fringe of the woods when May finally spoke. "*One change,*" she said, "*changes everything.*"

"Uh," said Cecily.

May looked at her. "Mr Lockwood said that if the princes hadn't died in the Tower, Jeremy might not have run away."

"But they did. Die in the Tower."

"But maybe they didn't. Maybe they got taken to Snow Castle. And died there, instead."

The woods, whispery, shady, close, released the children into the green light of the far field. To be speaking of ghosts under such sunlight felt absurd, like building a dungeon into a doll's house. Cecily didn't say that her uncle was given to fanciful ideas, which Heloise always advised her daughter to ignore. She said, "But even if they did go to Snow Castle, it would still mean Jeremy would run away – wouldn't it? *Whatever* happened back then still ends with Jeremy running away."

It was perhaps the most logical thing May had ever heard her say, so she ignored it as an exception to the rule. "Why don't you go back to the house," she said, not completely unkindly. "Go back and sit with your mother. She's worried."

Fatigued in body, wounded in spirit, willing to do anything – even commune with ghosts – rather than sit with her mother, Cecily replied, "I think I should come with you. I don't think you should go alone."

May snorted. "Those boys won't hurt anyone. They especially won't hurt me."

Cecily didn't ask why; she just followed. Satiny birds flew about, silver grass glistened. The earth blew wet bubbles under the pressure of the children's footsteps. They reached the river and Cecily, arms windmilling, groaned as water sloshed into her shoes. May, of course, crossed easily and without incident, as if she'd been born to ford streams.

And then Snow Castle was before them, the river humming behind them, the gigantic sky above. The walls of the castle, decorated by weeds and smirched by the mossy hands of years, folded around each other like a stony house of cards stilled in mid-collapse. Fleetingly, Cecily thought the ruins beautiful, not for what they had been, but for what they were. Eerily beautiful, like gossamer. Grandly tragic, like a mausoleum. Then the ruins became ruined again, and the sky was empty of birds, and the only sound came from a sullen drip that had been dripping for years.

And in the midst of it sat the brothers, close to each other, cross-legged on the ground, their faces turned only slightly as if they'd seen and heard the girls coming but were pretending they had not. They looked as real as life, as real as blood and time. "Hello," said May.

The boys dipped their heads; the youngster smirked. They seemed to be holding small things in their hands, pebbles or chips of marble. Their long hair blew about their white throats.

"Hello?" May shifted her feet. "Can you see us?"

The child, unable to contain himself, gave a giggle, and shushed it. "Don't look," the girls heard him whisper hotly to himself.

They were surely real, for only real boys could be so aggravating. "We can see you," said Cecily. "Don't act silly."

The child harrumphed and twisted, flinging open his hands. Tiny black stones flew through the air, disappearing as soon as they touched the ground. "Why do you always come here?" he asked, rude as ever.

"We want to see you," said May.

"No one is supposed to see us. I've told you this before." The older brother turned his head. He still looked ill, but not iller. A fussy boy, his velvet clothes were as prim as always. "Anyway, just because you *want* to see us doesn't give you the right to do so. We decide whom we shall and shan't see."

Cecily said blandly, "Well we can see you."

"We need your help," said May.

The boy gazed at the girls. Seated in the dirt, his cloak rucked around him, he looked like an exquisite puppet who'd been dropped on to the floor. Surprising them, he said, "There is grief between you – you, and you. You have been hurting each other."

"No we haven't," said Cecily.

"It's all right now," said May. "We've stopped."

"Good. You have been sent here together, as we have. Forgive. Forget."

"We *have*," Cecily assured him.

"We've come because we need your help," May said again.

"Mine?" The boy's lip curled. "I can't help you. I am no help to anyone. In everything I've tried, I have failed."

"You've looked after your brother all this time," Cecily pointed out, adding, "Better than I've looked after mine."

"Cecily's brother has run away," May explained. "We think he's gone to London."

The boy glanced at his sibling who had risen to his knees, watchful as a blackbird. "What has this to do with us? It has nothing to do with us."

"Everything is connected." May whispered the words like an incantation which would unlock an unseen door; and indeed the brothers twitched as if she'd trodden on their toes. "We are here because you are here."

Cecily hesitated, then edged a step closer, hands clasped under her chin. She really didn't know what to believe about these boys. Though their voices were clear and their clothing elaborate and their curls and pink skin soapily clean and alive, there came from them a feeling of thinness, as if they existed under a cold blue light and could not step away from its beam. There came from them a nothingness that was like the air in a cave. She couldn't believe, but she could believe. She drew a breath and said, "It does have something to do with you. You're children, just like us – just like all children, ever. You're frightened and brave, but other children are frightened and brave too. May is. The children in London, they are. You've never been the only ones to feel this way."

"I think," said the boy, "we have been more frightened, and had to be braver, than most."

May bit her lip, peering over the stony distance that could not be crossed. "Jeremy wants to be as brave as you. That's why he ran away."

"He is good and gentle," said Cecily.

"He wants to do something noble—"

"A worthy ambition."

"– but it makes me worry we won't see him again. It's what happens sometimes. Sometimes, the noble thing is the last thing. And after that you never see the person again."

A breeze went around the ruins, tousled the brothers' long locks. The child shuffled close to whisper in his sibling's ear. The boy nodded, smiled sadly at the evacuee. "Is it Jeremy you wish returned," he asked, "or somebody else?"

"Him!" said Cecily. "Who else is there?"

236

May's heart was beating hard. She took a step forward, the earth clinging to her feet and trying to hold her back, not wanting its little girl to go. "You could find him, couldn't you? You could speak to him."

The child looked owlishly at his brother. The boy did nothing for a moment. Then he stated, "We can't leave here."

"Have you tried?"

"Don't ask me if I've tried! I tried my best every day of my life. We were sent here. We had no choice. We are watched. We cannot leave. We are imprisoned!"

The girls shied from his temper. The earth bubbled and wheezed. May said, "Where's your prison? I don't see it. All I see are fallen-down stones and weeds. There's no lock. There aren't any chains. You see something that doesn't exist."

"No one but us knows you're here," said Cecily. "No one is watching you except birds."

"You're not prisoners," May told them. "That's all finished. If you want to, you can just walk away."

The brothers stared. In the sunlight they wavered, grew milky, were solid again. The child squeezed the older boy's hand. "I would like to see Mama," he said.

His brother ignored him, muttered, "You speak as if it would be simple."

"It would be! Wouldn't it?"

"We are accustomed to this place. We are part of it now."

"But this is a sad forgotten place—"

"Is that how you want to be?" asked Cecily. "Sad and forgotten?"

"Please, brother," pleaded the younger one. "Let's escape! Let's adventure! I would rather a terrible adventure than to stay here for ever and ever."

The older boy smiled morosely, and turned away. If the wind blew cool through his linen shirt, he did not shiver. He looked back, and his grey eyes were tired and angry. "And if we did as you say and left this place, and if, in our travels, we were to see this boy Jeremy, what are we to do with him?"

"Send him home!" yelped Cecily.

"Protect him," said May.

The boys glanced at each other. "I want to see Mama," the smaller said again.

The elder winced with indecision. "If we leave here, we must go far, far," he said. "It might be dangerous. And I am duty-bound to keep my brother safe."

"You do keep him safe," said Cecily. "Look at him, he's well. He's almost too well. You'll always know how to keep him safe. You're the big brother."

The boy's shoulders fell; he reluctantly smiled. He looked into his sibling's eager face, reached out and closed his hand around the child's paw. "If we leave this place," he said, "it will mean accepting there is nothing for us here, and that we must say goodbye. But we are only children. I don't mind for myself, but – my brother is a little child. He should have been allowed to stay, and grow up, and grow old, as others

238

have done. It isn't fair. It isn't the way it's promised to be."

He wiped his hand across his face, a hand which was ghostly in its delicacy, a face like that of a grieving angel. May and Cecily watched with paining hearts. The decrepit drip of water dripped – paused – dripped – paused again. The child hung his head in a silence deeper than a sea.

It was May who spoke. "Isn't it better to say goodbye and go, than to stay as prisoners forever? Isn't it better to leave a place where you don't belong?"

The boy shook his head hopelessly. His brother shuffled near until their knees touched. When the boy lifted his face, his eyes were filled with tears. Cecily had the strange thought that the tears were like diamonds, ancient and cold. "We are afraid to leave," he confessed. "*I* am afraid. Life was one way, and suddenly it was another. There was light, and then there was not. Nothing can be trusted. It has made me afraid."

May said, "I don't think you need to be afraid. I think you'll be safe. I think you'll be much happier when you've left this lonely place. You've stayed here too long, and it's made you too sad. But if you are scared about going, I can ask my dad to look after you."

The boy smiled, pressed a tear away. "There are countless souls in need of comfort," he said. "History is lined with the likes of them. How would he find us amid so many?"

"I don't know how," May replied, "but he would do it. He always found me in a crowded place. He never let me get lost."

The child jiggled his brother's hand. "Let's go," he

pleaded, "let's go. Let's go see Mama. Let's go adventuring. I want to sail the ocean. I want to run and run."

But instead the boy looked around at the ruins, and Cecily wondered what he saw: the walls and doors and carpets and ceilings of a prison built five centuries ago, or the welcoming blue sky that had been there since the earth was born out of darkness. "Is it truly all right to leave?" he asked.

"I think so."

"The weather seems fine. Cool, but the sun shines."

"A good day for travelling," said Cecily.

"If we go, it will be because we want to. Not because you say we should."

"That's all right. We know that."

"No one may tell us what to do!" remembered the bumptious child.

"Not any more," agreed May.

"We shall think on it," said the boy: yet already the brothers had risen like smoke to their feet as if the mere thought of leaving was taking them away, leaving without further lingering as if they'd waited such a long time to be told their time had passed, and they were free. "If you see my dad," May rushed to say, "tell him I miss him. Tell him I won't forget him—" but they might not have heard, for they were already gone in spirit and perhaps could not hear. And although their backs were to her, May did the singular thing that Cecily would never forget: she bowed.

A HERO FOUND

Three days later, Jeremy was home. His father – more precisely, a man who did as Jeremy's father commanded, for Humphrey Lockwood was occupied with war business at that particular junction in time – put him on the train and sent him back to Heron Hall. He was met at the village station by Hobbs, who gave him a small stone figurine which was the trophy of his dirt-stained collection.

If anyone expected Jeremy to be ashamed of his behaviour, they were disappointed. Indeed, any criticism of the boy was silenced at the sight of him. Apart from some scuffing of his hands, his escapade hadn't harmed him: but in his thin face and dark eyes was a new look, a fine look, a proud and peaceful look. If anyone had said anything sharp to him, the look on his face suggested he would smile and agree, because agreement would make the speaker happy; but that the speaker, smiled-upon and agreed-with in this easy way, would be left feeling narrow-minded and petty. The household came to stare at him, this boy who had run off as a naughty child and returned with the air of a prophet.

The train journey had not tired him, for, though he seemed like somebody else now, Jeremy was still fourteen, with energy to spare. He ate supper in Peregrine's den under the curious gaze of his family. Heloise could not take her eyes from this stranger who was her son. He would grow up to become what she hoped he'd be, a most respected and honoured man, a lawyer and, eventually, a judge; yet he did this not for her but for himself, because he returned to Heron Hall wanting to make a worthy difference to the world. In running away, he had lost the dreams of childhood and found some of the truths that make a man. He would always keep that stone figurine close to him, on a shelf where he could see it.

When he'd left Heron Hall five days earlier, it had been in the darkest hours; by the time Cecily found his note and empty bed, Jeremy had been miles away. "You must have known I'd be worried," said Heloise, and Jeremy replied, "Well, Mother, I left you the note saying you shouldn't be." And the tone of his voice, so sedate and reasonable, forced Heloise to admit that yes, he had left such a note saying just such a thing, and she really should have paid it more attention. The boy who sat before them was clearly capable of looking after himself. She'd always seen him as a flailing child, and he wasn't like that at all.

Throughout that first day he had walked, climbing stiles and crossing meadows, avoiding the roads. He'd known that people might be searching for him, and he hadn't wanted to be found. He had walked and walked, but he hadn't got far; hiking was a slow way to travel. He had slept that night in a barn – "Ha!" cried Cecily. "Did you really sleep in a barn? Just like a tinker! I *told* you, didn't I, Mama?" – and after a spiny night in the straw he'd risen at pink daybreak and found a road, a passing lorry, and caught the first of several lifts which carried him, in fits and starts, south towards London. Eventually he was able to catch a train, arriving on the outskirts of the city around four o'clock, just as the day was closing in on itself. As the train wended its path underground he saw that people were using the stations as places of refuge from the bombs. Already women, children and elderly folk were readying themselves for the night, laying out their beds of tartan blankets on the dirty platforms. When he'd stepped off the train he had to pick his way carefully, not wanting to trample fingers or leave a bootprint where someone might sleep.

He found the stairs, the pointy-finger exit signs, and came up from the underground, out into the world.

The clean green fields and watercolour sky of the countryside were gone. This was a brown and black world, the air a dusty grey. People in hats and summer coats walked the streets as they had always done, and there was even a feeling of good cheer, as on Christmas Eve when the stores have closed and there's nothing to do but wait for morning. Women wore high heels, men carried briefcases, bicycles and cars wove past on the road. But the grey dust touched everything, swirled in the wake of vehicles, cascaded down the shoulders of men. Where women had walked, the dust on the path preserved a trail of scratchy heel-marks. He had felt it on his teeth, that dust. It settled on his lips and tasted of all the centuries it had taken to build the city.

Rounding a corner, Jeremy caught his breath. The road was strewn with rubble, broken bricks and shattered timbers, huge plates of plaster. A sagging row of shopfronts lined the street, each of them missing its glass. In one yawning hole which had once been a window, a chalked sign said *Business As Usual.* Other stores looked abandoned, their window displays raided. Looking up, he saw that the shops had been scalped of their roofs. Water poured out of a burst pipe. Debris crunched underfoot.

He walked for as long as the light held, choosing his direction randomly. People filled the streets as the working day came to an end. They waited at bus-stops, scooted by on bikes, hurried with their colleagues to the underground. Some talked and smiled, others kept their heads down. Some stopped to consider the great blast-holes in the footpaths, the buildings torn from the rows, the piles of metal and brick that heaped chunderously over the roads. But most people did not stop, gave the destruction barely a glance. They had seen these things before, and in the morning there would be fresh things to see.

As evening closed in, creeping coldly through the dust, the streets emptied as if they'd had the life shaken from them. He had reached a suburban road now, and the houses that stood here were undamaged, and probably there were people living unremarkably inside them: but the homes seemed to turn to Jeremy the faces of haunted houses, gutted and long unloved. Their windows were messily blacked with tape, board, fabric. Their doors were shut as if nailed to their frames. Not a dog barked, no insect thrummed, the trees didn't shift a leaf. That untouched street, Jeremy realized later, was the scariest place he saw. Like a prisoner pegged out on a beach, it was waiting resignedly for whatever must happen.

Darkness drifted shyly in. Taverns turned out their lights. The few people who were still on the streets paid Jeremy no mind. Everyone knew what was coming, and what must be done. Everyone assumed he was on his way to shelter *somewhere safe*. But he had left that place of somewhere safe, and as night sunk around him he thought of all the boys who had gone before him, the ones who endured fearsome trials on desert plains, in frail canoes, on horseback, in the heart of jungles, on the rims of volcanos; trials of pain, confusion, skill, wisdom, strength and, most of all, of courage; harrowing tests of a boy's worthiness of becoming a warrior. Jeremy wanted to spend this night outside, as far as possible from *somewhere safe*. Himself against the bombs: he craved it.

Heloise, listening to this, shook her head with a mother's mournful pride. All around the world that night, other mothers, learning of the fatal boldness of their own sons, would do the same.

"I walked for a long time," Jeremy told his listeners. "I wasn't hungry or thirsty, I wasn't even cold. I didn't know when the bombing would start, I didn't know where to go. No place seemed a more likely target than another. So I just kept walking and hoped for the best."

"Hoped for the best!" spluttered Heloise. "Hoped to be standing where a bomb might fall!"

Jeremy ignored her with the patience of one whose calling cannot be explained. "Finally I found a garden and sat down. I fell asleep – not completely asleep, but asleep enough that the silliest thoughts made sense. When I heard the siren, I thought I was back in school and the bell was ringing to call us to class. Then I remembered the bell had never sounded as urgent as that."

He'd opened his eyes to the oddest of sights: the sky above him was red. It was slashed across with the white beams of searchlights, and burnt black at the edges by night: but the clouds were red as if the sky had been drenched by buckets of blood.

He didn't see aeroplanes, but he felt the vibrations shake

through his body, four hefty booms to the chest as the bombs drove themselves into the ground.

"I started running. The sirens were howling. There was a big moon, a hunter's moon, so I could see where I was going. I passed other people, and most of them were wearing gas masks and helmets. I didn't have a helmet or a mask, but I didn't care. I wasn't frightened – not frightened at all. I felt almost . . . mad. I couldn't wait to get to the place where the bombs had hit. I was punching my legs as I ran, trying to make them run faster. I felt *sick* with excitement, *crazy* with it – not excited to see the damage, but *to be there*. I felt I was running as fast as the wind, but even that wasn't fast enough. I felt I could break bricks in my hands, that's how furious I was. I felt like . . . a lion."

His eyes were glassy recalling it: Cecily stared at this changed, slightly worrying brother of hers. She glanced at Peregrine, who was watching him also. There was no astonishment on her uncle's face; rather, he looked as if he'd just been told that all cats have claws.

The bomb site was a mile away. He was led to it by the fires that reached for the scarlet sky, by the shrilling of ambulances and fire trucks, by the dust that billowed along the roads as a thick, repellent snow. When he reached the place, the sight was shocking. A row of seven terrace houses had been pulled down as if by a mudslide. A ravaged mountain of doors, walls, gutters and furniture spewed into the street. Chimneys were standing, as were odd walls;

staircases reached for rooms that were no longer there. He wasn't the first to arrive at the scene – there were men with hoses and first-aid kits, women with crowbars and stretchers, as well as people who had dredged themselves from the wreckage and were now digging for their entombed families and neighbours. Instructions were being shouted, whistles being blown, torch beams were clashing like sabres in the night. Something caught fire, blew a ball of flame into the sky; the rescuers answered it gruffly, neither impressed nor afraid.

Jeremy did what all boys in search of achievement must do: he left the crowd to find an arena of his own, a private stage. He doubled back the way he had come, located a lane and followed it to the rear of the bombed terrace. There were fewer people working here in the tight confines of the toppled fences and buckled concrete and smithereened privies, and none of them noticed the blond boy who had never walked these working-class streets before, who had no idea what he was doing, who knew only what he wanted to do.

"I started digging. Well, *digging* isn't the word. It was more like clearing a path between the slabs of plaster and chunks of wall and the pieces of tile, hoping to come across something – *someone*. Broken bricks were everywhere, in rough stinking piles. I could smell gas, and I could hear people in the street, and the sirens were still wailing, meaning more bombs might be on their way; but I didn't think about that. I didn't think about anything except *doing something*. I pushed and pulled at the rubble, kicked it, climbed over it, crawled under it, swore at it, I went at it in a fury; and *I had* to do it, *I had* to conquer the wreckage, as if my kicking and smashing through it was somehow *hurting* the enemy. As if Hitler himself could sense my determination and see that he might as well give up now, because he was never going to win. . ."

Jeremy looked up with burning eyes. He evidently felt no embarrassment in admitting to such anarchy of feeling, and in fact seemed pleased by it. He smiled at himself with a kind of wondering delight. "Do you think I was mad? I felt mad. I feel a little mad just telling you the story. I felt – I still feel – that I hardly know the person I am. And it makes me happy, feeling that.

"I was working by myself – nobody was near me. The moon was big and white, you could see the dust rising against the sky. I was dragging an angle of timber like a guillotine frame when I heard a noise. I knew what it was straight away. Somebody was calling for help. People were under the rubble, and they were pounding on something, and crying for help."

Quickly his keen ears had pinpointed the direction of the sound. It was coming from close to where he stood – to where his feet perched precariously on a floe of shattered tiles. The voices were coming from an underground cellar. Instantly all was clear to him: the inhabitants of the terrace had used their cellar as a bomb shelter. They had survived the blast, but their home had not; and now they were trapped by the weight of the debris.

"I didn't call anyone over: everyone was busy, but I also wanted the rescue to be mine – I wanted to do it. That's why I was there. I started throwing aside all sorts of rubbish, coat-hangers, shoes, a hatstand, an alarm clock; I remember pulling an apron out of the dirt, and it still had a house key pinned to it. I was working fast, without having to think, as if I'd been born to dig like a mole. I uncovered the cellar door in no time. It wasn't a wooden door, as I'd expected, but a sheet of thick steel, a true air-raid-shelter door. In the moonlight I could see where it had been freshly welded into place. It wasn't set flat into the ground, but tilted at an angle; there must have been stairs behind it leading down into the room. I banged on the steel with my fist, to show the trapped people I was there. They answered with a frenzy of pounding. There was a handle, and I pulled at it – and the door didn't budge. I could tell it was a heavy door, but that wasn't the problem. Something had buckled it, and now it would not open.

"I looked around for a lever, thinking that would work. Finding a good one took me a minute. All that time the people in the cellar were hammering on the door. I imagined them in the darkness, and knew it would be unpleasant, but I did think they were making an impatient fuss. I found a nice piece of timber and applied it to the door. I struggled with it, put all my weight on it, but I couldn't get the door to budge. I could hear voices behind the steel, but whatever they were saying was blurred. I assumed they were saying *help, help, get us out*. Well, that was what I intended to do, if they'd give me a moment. Sirens were still ringing, and hoses were spraying water, and fires were burning here and there; it was difficult to hear anything clearly. But suddenly I did hear something, a man's voice from behind the steel, a deep hard voice that might have belonged to an oak tree. *Hurry*, he said. *The cellar is flooding.*"

May, who had been silent so far, said, "Oh." They had read of such things in the newspapers. The bombs ripped apart the underground water mains; and people, trapped by rubble in their cellars and basements, drowned.

"As soon as I realized what he was saying, I started pulling frantically at the door. I looked up once or twice, hoping someone would be close enough to help me, but no one was near, I was completely on my own, I found out later that they'd discovered a lady trapped inside a chimney, and everyone had run to see. I didn't want to leave my people in the cellar, not even for a second. I couldn't bear to turn my back on them. I couldn't bear the thought of not being able to find them again amid all the muck and dark and ruin. *Help!* I started yelling. *Help! Help me over here!* But with all the busyness, the trucks and the sirens, nobody noticed me.

"The people in the cellar were hammering wildly now. The door only seemed to wedge tighter with every thump it received. I was pulling, and they were pushing, but we

251

may as well have been trying to move a mountain-range. Several times I heard the oak-tree man shout the word *water*. And once, when I glanced about for help, I noticed water leaking from cracks in the concrete in the yard behind me. Somewhere beneath us must have been a great pipe, torn to pieces like everything else. When I saw that water leaking across the yard, I knew the situation was bad. I knew the cellar must be filling fast. I knew it would be a small room, the cellar, a low-ceilinged, windowless room, and that this door was the last way out.

"By now, the people in the cellar were screaming. They were screaming and shouting at me. *Hurry up! Get us out! Hurry up!* I couldn't hear the words clearly, the door was very thick; but I could hear their fists beating, and each beat said those things. *Hurry up. We're going to die. You came here to save us. Now, because of you, we're going to die.*

"I started screaming in reply. In the dark, in the panic, I wasn't myself any more. I felt as if I had no body, only a mind and a whirlwind of feeling. I wasn't frightened. I was enraged. I was enraged at myself, because those people were right: I'd come to save them but I couldn't do it, and now they would die. I was lowly, I was nothing, I'd imagined myself someone special yet all I was was a wretch who couldn't even open a door. I yelled and yelled for help, and I hauled and hauled at the door, but it didn't budge, and then a terrible thing happened: water seeped out past the bottom edge of the door. I noticed it instantly, as if I'd searched my whole life to see it. It sputtered out at first, then started to leak steadily. I wasn't certain, but I guessed it meant the flooding was at least up to the shoulders of someone like the oak-man. I imagined children in that watery death-crawling darkness; I thought of you, Cecily, and you too, May. And I thought – and this shows how mad I must have been, to be thinking something like this at a time like that – of those two boys in the Tower, the princes. I saw, in my mind, all these children behind doors, and I wanted to scream, and perhaps I did. And a voice in my head started saying, *You're not the first. You're not the first who couldn't open a door,* and although that could have been consoling, it wasn't. I didn't want to be another boy behind a locked door. *I had* to set these people free. *I could not* let this awful thing happen over and over again. *I could not* let wrongness and cruelty and greed and – *power* – win."

He halted his telling and chewed his lip, as if the telling had got away from him and he had to reel the tale in. He looked at his uncle, smiled weakly. "That's exactly what I thought: *I could not let power win.* As if power is an enemy with arms and eyes and legs, capable of carrying a gun or throwing a grenade – capable of bending a steel door until it jammed shut. *Get away from here, you wicked thing*: that's what I wanted to say to power. *You bring nothing but despair, as if you utterly despise everyone, even the smallest and most innocent.* This is what I really thought, standing in a blown-up yard in the middle of the night, wrestling useless as

253

a flea at a door while the people behind it drowned. Talking to power as if power could hear me and cared the least for what I had to say. I tell you, I was mad. I was insane. I had lost my mind.

"The water was leaking past the door in a wide thin river now. My shoes were wet, I left wet footprints on the metal when I kicked the door. I glanced up and saw some men at the end of the lane. I yelled to them but they didn't see me. There was so much mess, so much smoke, so much noise. The oak-man was hollering, and pounding at the door, and even though I wasn't listening to what he was saying, I also knew I would never stop hearing it. *Even when I am an old man,* I thought, *I will hear the sound of fists on closed doors.* And that thought was like a ton of bricks coming down on my shoulders. It made me stagger and fall over in the dust. And when I was lying there on the glass and concrete, I had another funny thought. I thought about those princes again, who'd died before they'd hardly lived. I thought about the Duke. I thought, The Duke was a king, but it was those boys who ruled him, and have ruled him for five hundred years, and will always rule him. I thought, *You think a child has no power, but you're wrong.*

"And so I stood up, and I took hold of the door, and I pulled against it as I had been doing all along – and it opened so easily that I fell again. It *threw* me aside, and I fell down on my behind, and water rushed out of the cellar, and so did the people. Seven people came running into the dark, three of them children still being carried high as if their parents couldn't trust the grey air not to turn to black water. I couldn't tell which was the oak-man. All of them were shadows, all of them were soaked to the skin. Not one stopped or looked about. They came out like animals from Noah's ark, like souls rushing up from a grave. They were crying. They were screaming. They didn't notice me. They just ran and ran, into the lane, into the night, into somewhere that wasn't where they had been."

Jeremy stopped; he seemed weary now. His dark eyes searched the pattern on the rug. "I wasn't sure what to do then," he sighed. "I lay in the muck, panting and looking at the sky, waiting for someone to find me, or cheer for me, or lift me up. But no one even saw me, and after a while I realized that no one had to. Something remarkable had happened, seven lives had been saved, three children would grow up, grow old – but that was already in the past. Other remarkable things had to happen now, a whole string of remarkable things, one after another until the war was won. I was small, and I'd only done one small thing, really: but still it was a mighty thing. Mightier than what power was doing, with its bombs and guns. It was something great. It was . . . enough."

He looked at his audience, and smiled in the hesitant but certain way in which he would always smile, from this moment until the end of his long and well-lived life. Byron, stretched out on the carpets, waved his flag of tail.

WHAT IS TRUE

There were things to be done: Jeremy wanted to return to school, he wanted to start readying himself for the future right away, he was happy to go abroad if his mother and father thought it necessary. It was high time Cecily and May were also sent to school – the village school would suffice for the time being, but if the war dragged on then Cecily, at least, must be sent somewhere more suited to a girl of her class and degree of laziness. Cecily's shoulders slumped: it was typical that her brother should run away and throw the household into chaos, but that it should be she, an innocent party, who bore the severest punishment.

All this would be arranged over the days to follow: for now it was time for the children to take their baths and go to bed. "I'm very relieved to have you home." Heloise smoothed her boy's hair. "I'm going to try to forget this unpleasantness ever happened." Jeremy said nothing, only smiled at her; but in his eyes was a pity that would never wear away.

Peregrine's legs were clearly hurting him badly after the stress of the last few days, but he stood and offered his nephew his hand. "I'm glad to have you home," he said, "but I'm also glad you went."

"I'm sorry if I've caused you trouble, Uncle. But I had to go."

"I know it," said Peregrine.

The girls tailed their returned soldier up the everest of stairs. They followed him all the way to his bedroom, where new linen had been laid on the bed, and fresh pyjamas and slippers, a clean towel and a face-cloth were set out on the chair. The girls stopped in the doorway, jostling each other. "Jem," said Cecily, "can we ask you something?"

"If you like."

Cecily bumped May with her elbow. "Ask him."

May went to speak, but hesitated; Jeremy looked at her. "What is it, May?"

The girl took a steadying breath and said, "When you were walking around the city, did you – see anyone strange? Maybe – feel anything strange?"

"Everything was strange. What do you mean?"

"Did anyone come near you, or speak to you? Two boys?"

"Two boys?" He frowned. "No. No one spoke to me. No one took any notice of me."

"What about when you were trying to open the cellar door? Did you feel anything – helping you? A voice telling you to keep going, or some strange strength inside you – something that wasn't you?"

Jeremy, sitting on the bed to unlace his shoes, paused. "Do you mean like God, or an angel?"

"Yes," said May, "angels. That's what I mean."

Jeremy slipped the shoe from his foot, let it drop bluntly to the floor. He thought about the question for some moments, long enough to raise the expectations of the girls. Then he said, "No. I didn't feel anything like God or angels. All I felt was anger. I was angry that things happen which shouldn't happen. I was angry that *might equals right*. Because it doesn't. It never does. And being angry gave me strength. That's what told me to keep going. Not a heavenly thing – a human thing."

"Hmm," said May.

Cecily asked, "What did you do after the people ran from the cellar like animals out of the ark?"

Jeremy began work on the knotted lace of his other shoe. "I picked myself up. I dusted myself off. I should have stayed to help, I suppose, but somehow I knew I'd done everything I was meant to do and that if I stayed I would just be getting under the rescuers' feet. So I started to walk. I was wet and dirty and worn out. It must have been close to midnight. The sirens were stopping and starting. The sky was still red, and the planes were still coming, but they weren't near where

I was any more. I hadn't had much to eat, and I suddenly started thinking about food. I thought about roast-beef sandwiches – you know how Mrs Potter always makes them for us, Cec, with the top slice of bread dunked in gravy."

"Oh!" Cecily clapped her hands to her face.

"Suddenly roast-beef sandwiches were all I could think about. I was miles from home, but I started running, almost flying, as if the thought of a roast-beef sandwich was a magic carpet. I just swooped all the way home. It must have taken an hour, but it seemed like minutes. I wasn't tired or puffed at all. In the blink of an eye, I was home."

"Daddy." Cecily whispered it between her fingers.

"The house looks exactly as it did when we left it. No bombs have fallen on the neighbourhood. The windows were still blacked, the streetlights were switched off. But there was a gap in the curtains of Father's study, and a line of light was shining through it. I knew he'd left that gap in the curtains, that light burning, for me."

With muffled joy Cecily said, "Ah!"

"I knocked on the door, and Mr Mills let me in. We didn't say much to each other, he said he would fetch some tea and ask Mrs Potter about the sandwich. It felt odd to be home again. Everything was the same, but I felt like a visitor seeing things for the first time. Everything felt as if it had been placed there for me to admire, but that if I touched it I would discover it was all made of cardboard, like props built for the stage."

Cecily frowned; she didn't want May getting the impression she lived in a house decorated by cardboard.

"I went upstairs to Father's study. I was nervous, I tell you. I knew I looked a mess. I knew I would be in strife. I'd been wilful and caused trouble, when everyone had enough to worry about. Fa might be interested to hear my story, he might even be proud of what I'd done: but I knew I was in for a talking-to, at the very least. So I was nervous, but also happy. I was looking forward to seeing him, and having him to myself for a while. We could talk seriously, like men, about my plans. About his work. About the war."

He had untied and taken off his other shoe and now let it slide from his fingers to the floor, where it landed with a bump beside its twin.

"I knocked on the door, and there was no answer, so I turned the handle and walked in. I expected Father to be at his desk, wearing that expression he always has when we interrupt his work – very cross, but also very pleased, as if he'd been interrupted on the verge of some decision he didn't want to make. So my face was turned to the desk as I walked into the room. And he wasn't there – his chair was empty – papers and pens were there, and the typewriter and a coffee cup, and the chair was pushed away from the desk, and the lamp was burning – but Father wasn't there. So I turned to leave, and that's when I saw him, lying on the couch at the other end of the room. Stretched out in his socks and braces, sound asleep on the couch."

"Daddy," sighed Cecily. "Poor old Daddy."

"Poor Daddy?" said her brother. "That is not what I thought. I thought, *Who are you? What are you doing there, asleep?* Bombs are dropping all over the city, houses are being blown to pieces, people are being buried alive. In battlefields across Europe men are holed up in darkness, listening to the enemy marching closer and closer. Men are shooting each other out of the sky, languishing in war camps, bleeding to death in no-man's-land. Old people are huddled in train stations, children are hiding under kitchen tables listening to the scream of sirens and the whistle of bombs and wondering if it's the last thing they'll ever hear. Women are lifting their neighbours off the road and into morgue trucks. Men are climbing into aeroplanes that they know can't fly faster than their enemy's. All of it was happening as I stood there in the doorway. Yet here was Fa, asleep on his couch. Never going near a battlefield, never living among the rats and the wreckage. Never queuing for rations. Never laying out blankets on a platform. Never finding a baby orphaned in its cradle. Never writing a letter to a mother, telling her her son was dead. No. There he was, collar unbuttoned, sound asleep."

"Jem," said Cecily quietly.

He ignored her. "So that's what I thought: *Who are you, Father?* I thought you were grand. I thought you were good. But you're not those things. I thought you were noble, majestic: but you're just a coward, like all those who stand behind the suffering of others. Sleeping while other people's lives come to an end at your command."

"Jem!" cried his sister, scandalized.

"And then he must have sensed me in the room, because he opened his eyes. Immediately he was Fa again. He sat up and said, *What a welcome visitor.* He said, *I hear you've come home to win the war.* And what could I do, then, but love him? You know how he is: you *must* love him. You have no choice in the matter, it's impossible to resist. Around Fa, some things just have to be."

Jeremy had discarded his socks by now, revealing bony feet which he looked at as though he could choose others if these ones didn't appeal. "I have to take my bath," he said, "before the water goes cold."

"All right," muttered Cecily. "Goodnight, Jem."

"You're not going to run away again, are you?" asked May.

"No." He smiled. "I'll see you in the morning."

Thus dismissed, the girls went into the hallway and drifted toward their bedrooms. Cecily's chest felt as if a band of iron was bound around it: every time she tried to breathe she remembered her brother's description of her sleeping father, and the air seemed to jam in her lungs. She loved her father, *loved him*, and he had a perfect right to sleep . . . but how she wished that he had been awake that night. How she wished it. She felt a forlorn sadness and didn't yet know it was just the sadness of growing up.

At her door, she touched May's sleeve. "Wait," she said. "I'm sorry about your daddy, May."

May's eyes flashed. They had not yet spoken of this. Cecily had been muted by guilt – so often she had bragged and reminisced about her father, and never once thought to ask why May kept such a soft silence about her own – and had hoped the subject would be lost amid the peculiarity of the past days; but it wouldn't. "Thank you," said May.

"Did he die in a battle?"

The girl shook her head. "He was missing. Then we got a telegram saying he'd been killed."

Cecily nodded. "He must have been very brave," she said.

May glanced at the rugs, the balustrades, the ivory walls. She drew a deep breath and let it out. "Sometimes I can't remember his face," she admitted. "Sometimes I can hardly remember anything about him."

"Well. . . You remember the names of birds and trees. You remember what he taught you about history and paintings. You remember the stuffed animals at the museum, don't you?"

"Yes."

"I think that means you can remember your dad."

May considered this. "Thank you," she said again.

"We'll win the war," said Cecily, "because of him."

"Yes." May smiled. "I know."

They did not know that the war would lash the world

for nearly six long years, scraping millions into its maw; they didn't know that May would spend these years in the embrace of Heron Hall, becoming a daughter of the house and a precious almost-daughter to Peregrine; or that, long after her mother had taken her to live on the opposite side of the world, May would write letters to Peregrine, and often think about him; nor that, after he died, she would receive a delicate gold locket inside which was the portrait of a sombre man wearing a fine cloak and many jewels, whose eyes seemed full of regret. They didn't know that Cecily would grow up to have three good sons of her own and that she would live a long and sunshine-filled life, growing frail and forgetful only in the last months of it, like a butterfly closing its wings. But that night, the two girls stood on the landing and nodded, sure in the knowledge of this one thing. They would win, because of him.

And during those years when Cecily and May grew up, what was left of Snow Castle crumbled and fell gently to pieces, and disappeared into the ground.